Pangatango's
Secrets

LELAND SCOTT

Order this book online at www.trafford.com
or email orders@trafford.com

Most Trafford titles are also available at major online book retailers.

Print information available on the last page.

ISBN: 978-1-4907-9167-8 (sc)
ISBN: 978-1-4907-9166-1 (hc)
ISBN: 978-1-4907-9168-5 (e)

Library of Congress Control Number: 2018912481

Trafford rev. 10/31/2018

www.trafford.com
North America & international
toll-free: 1 888 232 4444 (USA & Canada)
fax: 812 355 4082

Thank you to Nora Martin

This book began as a dream writing project between two longtime friends and continued to completion because of the inspiration from that beginning. Thank You, Nora, for your ideas and encouragement in that beginning and the memory of that inspiration that lingered through the writing.

Chapter 1

The little plane bumped and jerked to an unsteady landing. He had arrived – Pangatango! It had been a long trip, but he had arrived! Sam had heard of the island once during his military stint, where he had served a brief and uneventful two years in the marines. He had traveled very little, but some of his buddies told of being stranded here once when they had been on their way to the Philippines. Their plane had had problems and they were forced to land on this tiny island in the Pacific – an island he couldn't even find on the map... They had to stay on the island while they waited for their plane to be repaired. The story they told was mostly of some bar that had given them free drinks, but they had also told him of the fact that it was a desolate island with few tourists, but a nice hotel, where they had stayed. He had thought little of it at the time, but now it sounded like just the place he wanted to be. It sounded like a perfect escape from all that was crowding in on him. Too much had happened in the past few months and he had to escape. He had to find a place where no one would try to tell him what to do or how to think. He had to find a place where no one or no thing would distract or influence him. After some searching, his travel agent had located the island that he hoped would be such a place. The travel agent had arranged connections with a couple of commercial airlines and an island hopping plane and rented a small cottage for him for a month in advance. It was here that he now found himself like a castaway – just what he wanted. Little did he know what awaited him on Pangatango.

The runway had been quite short and as his plane had finally settled on its tail wheel and jolted to a stop. Sam wondered how that Marine plane had been able to land there, but he guessed that anything was possible if the need was great enough. The plane turned and taxied to a spot closer to the buildings and the crew opened the door and lowered the steps to the ground. He climbed out of the plane, surveying his surroundings. The airport was very unassuming – a large hangar that looked like it had been left over from some military use, and a couple of smaller buildings that he suspected had been built to house private planes. On the tarmac, there were several small planes, a gas truck, and an ancient fire truck. In the far blue-grey distance, there was what looked like a volcanic mountain. He had seen it from the air – it seemed to be near the center of the island and was covered with trees. He reckoned it hadn't been active for hundreds of years. He had also seen from the air that there seemed to be little else on the island but the one town and a few scattered villages that looked like only tiny clusters of shacks. There was no sign of farming or industry. He supposed the natives lived mostly from the sea. He had seen one small, lazy-looking seaport where he suspected small cargo ships could come with supplies from the outside world, and perhaps a cruise ship might anchor on occasion. No one seemed to be too excited about his plane's arrival – or anything else, for that matter. No luggage carts rushed out to meet the plane. No one hurried to greet the passengers. None of the other few passengers seemed to be in a great hurry to get to any important appointment or meet any desperate schedule. He followed them toward what appeared to be the terminal in the center of a small grassy area surrounded by Palm trees.

The terminal consisted of a small, neat, white concrete block building with a corrugated tin roof. A large sign over the door said "Welcome to Beautiful Pangatango". There were a couple of benches outside, against the wall. A dog slept peacefully under one of the benches. A couple of little dark-skinned boys, dressed only in shorts, sat in the grass nearby, laughing and playing some kind of game with two sticks and a small wooden ball. A huge, beetle of some kind struggled aimlessly across his path. He stepped over it. A door marked 'Welcome' led to a large room with a ticket counter and a few more benches. In front of him on the opposite side of the room, was another open door, obviously leading out to the street. On a side wall were three doors marked

"Men" "Women" and "Office".

"That about covers it", Sam mumbled to himself.

Opposite the ticket counter in a corner, was another small counter with a sign hanging overhead bearing the word 'Customs'. Several people sat here and there on benches or on the floor, chatting. One noisy tourist in a suit stood at the ticket counter, expounding his desire to charter a plane to somewhere... a nicely dressed woman stood quietly a few paces away with two expensive looking suitcases. She apparently was with the noisy one, but maintaining her distance from him. A few more people with assorted luggage seemed to be waiting for him to finish before approaching the counter where one slow-talking, attendant was trying to patiently soothe the noisy man. Sam was waved over to the 'Customs' counter by a stern looking man dressed in an official looking white shirt and dark trousers who asked him what he had in his bag. Sam looked down at the duffle bag he was carrying and replied, "Clothes". The official looked at Sam, smiled a broad smile with a wink and waved him past.

Outside, Sam stepped onto a palm lined street that led to the town and beyond. He could have walked the distance to the hotel – the only building over two stories high. It loomed less than two blocks away. But that was not his destination. As inviting as it may be, a hotel was definitely not where he wanted to be.

Uncertain of who he should ask directions of, Sam found three willing taxi drivers waiting… Their taxis were brightly painted jeeps, open-sided with colorful canvas tops. They were decorated with pom-poms and streamers and painted-on flowers and crosses. A statue of Jesus on the dashboard… Sam approached the first one in line and the driver motioned for him to climb in the back seat. He climbed in and handed the driver a card with the address of the cottage he had rented. The driver looked at it and silently nodded and immediately drove slowly away from the terminal.

Along their drive, which seemed to be the main street of the town, Sam quickly took in the view. The whole town may have been four blocks long, they passed the hotel and open-door shops and bars and markets of fruit, clothing, and tourist trinkets. The hotel stood like part of a movie set – three stories high with a pillared entrance and a portico like some majestic Southern Colonial mansion. Sam wondered at the sight of it – so out of place with all the simple buildings that followed. The hotel was surrounded by pots and beds of flowers and, behind the hotel, he could see flower-bordered lawns stretching out to a beach on a cove. There were a few tourist-looking people browsing the shops and walking along the street. There was a noticeable absence of cars. He saw only a few older ones, parked along side streets. The houses along the street looked well cared for and stood comfortably under palms and surrounded by flowers. He knew he would have to come back here to explore this town one day. But for now, he wanted to get as far as possible away from 'people and things' as he could.

They drove for only a short distance, passing the houses at the edge of town and then leaving town and along the shore, intermittently along an empty beach where he could see the waves pounding against the sand, and then away from the beach briefly and then returning to it again. Away from the beach, they drove between walls of thick brush. The brush looked similar to wild staghorn sumac at home, but without the bright leaves and berries. It had only sparse, dark, dry looking leaves. He wondered if this was the Mangrove plants he had heard of in the Caribbean. The road suddenly got narrower and narrower until it became only a one-lane sandy road. He wondered how people would pass if they met another car… no need to worry, he decided; there were no other cars.

Then, almost too soon, the driver stopped and pointed to a small cottage sitting alone some distance from the beach. "That's it" he said.

Sam asked, "How much?"

The driver said "Three dollars"

Sam gave him five.

The driver waved a smiling good-bye, turned around in the road and drove off. Sam was alone.

Sam walked the distance up a path of crushed shells and coral to the small building that the driver had pointed out. He wondered if he needed a key or something, but as he climbed the steps he found the door and windows open. It was a small building easily surveyed with a glance. The room he entered was living room, dining room and kitchen all in one. Through an open door, he saw a double bed in the bedroom and another door leading to a small bathroom. The furniture was sparse – the kitchen area had a counter with a sink and a small range, an ancient looking refrigerator, and some cupboards, above and below the counter. The rest of the room held a table, with four chairs, a rocker and an old wood framed couch with soft, flowered cushions. There was a lamp on a small table at one end of the couch, and a single light hanging on a cord over the table. A coffee table held a few old magazines and a large conch shell. The worn wooden floor was partially covered with an old oval rag rug. It looked simple, plain and un-pretentious, but cozy and welcoming. Sam sat down on the couch in the now dimming light of the afternoon and pulled off his shoes. He leaned back and closed his eyes and tried to collect his thoughts, remembering the day that had just passed.

He had left his hometown in Iowa some 21 hours earlier, flown half-way around the world to a small, almost primitive island in a search for something he was yet to identify. After his mother had died, he had been struggling with a lot of things. He thought briefly of her and the problems he had left behind and suddenly felt very tired. He grabbed his bag and moved to the bedroom; then to the bathroom. He fumbled with the shower and waited for hot water. It didn't come. He decided that cool water might feel good – and after a few seconds of conditioning his body to it, it did. It was a quick shower. He dried and went to bed. The bed was firm and inviting. The landlord had prepared it with sheets and a couple of pillows. A blanket lay folded over the footboard of the bed, but Sam didn't expect to need it. In spite of the breeze that drifted through the open windows, it was comfortably warm. He lay down, adjusted the pillow under his head and looking up at the rafters above, drifted off to sleep.

Chapter 2

With slow hesitant steps, Sam left the cabin and walked toward the water. The sun was just coming up and the beach looked deserted. He was glad. He didn't want to talk to anyone or even see anyone. Wearing only cut-off jeans and a T-shirt, he felt the misty air, but was sure he would be dressed warm enough for later in the day. He felt his bare feet settle into the cool sand with each step and paused briefly to feel the sand close over his toes before taking another step. There was the fishy seaweed smell in the air from the debris left by the receding tide. He didn't care. The aroma only added to his lonely, empty feeling. The slow lapping of incoming waves seemed to bring a melody to his thoughts. He stopped to look back at his tracks when he reached the wet, firmer sand. The tiny cottage he had rented was like a silhouette against the morning sky, and the foot prints leading to it seemed to blend into the scene creating something like one of those drawings that would be seen in some tourist shop. With an uncertainty, he began a walk that he hoped would help him define some thoughts that had been pounding at the inside of his head for weeks. He really didn't know what to expect or what he would solve by being here, but he had to try to think. He had to try to work some things out and make some decisions away from all the distractions of home.

Sam stooped to pick up a shell from the sand. He shook the sand from it and tumbled it carelessly in his hand without looking... The shell felt smooth and silky to his hand and as he rubbed the smoothness between his finger and thumb, his mind wandered to another shell on another beach a long time ago. He remembered a childhood trip with his older brother and parents to the Carolinas and the time they had spent at the ocean. It had been such a magical time – wading in the water and a picnic on a blanket on the sand. He remembered his mother and father so happy together, laughing beneath a beach umbrella while he built a sand castle at their feet. He remembered the shells, like this one, that he had gathered in a little pail to carry home. He remembered his disappointment when he had discovered, too late, that the pail had been left on the beach. He had cried quietly next to his sleeping brother in the back seat of the car on the way back to Iowa. He had cried as his parents laughed and chatted in the front seat, not noticing his sadness. He had forgotten about that incident until now! By the time they had gotten home, other things had become more important. How strange that it should suddenly reappear in his memory now. "How strange we are", Sam thought, "that we can forget and yet not really forget... things in our past are with us forever...". Sam pried open the door to the memories of his childhood. It had been a happy time - when the world was alright. What had happened? he wondered. Where had the world changed? His father was a good man. He had been a farmer, like his father before him. He had spent most of his life on the farm, tilling the Iowa soil and caring for the usual responsibilities of cattle and crops and family. Sam didn't remember his father ever getting very emotional about anything. He had been a man of invention and reaction. If things needed doing, he did them. Life had 'just happened'. Life had been good. His mother was a strong woman – with a physical strength necessary for a farm wife and a spiritual strength that displayed her convictions. She had been the moral backbone for the family. Sam and his brother, David, had been given attention by both mother and father; and he had willingly accepted both. He realized that his character had gained from both. His father had given him practical masculine strength and abilities. He could repair a broken piece of machinery or tend to an ailing animal with the same mechanical detachment and strength that his father had; but Sam could also appreciate the beauty of the sunset and sunrise, the flowers of the garden, and the smell of the apple blossoms that his mother had loved.

A gull swooped nearby, landed, and ran ahead of Sam along the beach, interrupting his thoughts of the past and returning him to the present. He turned his thoughts to the sand beneath his feet and the waves constantly surging, fading, and receding, absentmindedly watching the gull's movements and the tracks that it left in the sand. He felt a slight breeze against his face and the beginning of warm rays from the climbing sun. He shoved his hands deep into the pockets of his cut-off jeans and stretched his pace. Somehow, it seemed important to just walk. Looking neither to left or right, he followed the water's edge along the sandy beach concentrating on his own deliberate footsteps as though each step might lead him to that one perfect spot that he really could not yet define. He had no goal – only the purpose to just walk and think. Somehow he felt as though somewhere in this isolation he would find answers to the questions that plagued him. The cool sand and the sound of the waves seemed to shut out any distraction.

The gull turned suddenly toward the sea and took flight. With seemingly effortless action, it rose from the sand, raised its feet, and with a few flaps of wings was gracefully soaring above the waves. The slight movement of wingtips and feathers so gracefully and naturally controlled by this seemingly unintelligent creature made it a sight of beauty. It rose and fell on the currents of air in long sweeping circuits over the water. Sam paused to watch the miracle of flight and then resumed his own direction alone. He returned to the task of studying his footsteps – watching each foot make an imprint in the sand; which gently settled as the foot lifted, yet retaining an image of his foot. The shape of each toe and the contour of the sole of his foot, all so smoothly impressed in the damp sand. "How strange and wonderful we are to be able to walk and think and feel", he mused. He wondered if the other creatures, like the gull, ever considered their footsteps in the sand...ever saw amazement in flight...

Sam's thoughts raced in circles of childhood memories, his plane trip here, the flight of the gull, the sand and the breeze and the magnitude of it all... "There are no answers, only more mysteries," he thought...

The sun had risen from the faint misty sunrise to a warm brightness when Sam settled to rest on a large piece of driftwood half buried in the sand. He looked out at the sea and the rolling waves, wondering at the vastness of it all. It seemed so endless. Each wave would roll toward the shore, fall, and be no more - only to be followed by another. Each wave seemed to come from some far-away place intent on reaching the shore, with almost a characteristic of life – charging, pushing, reaching... but falling just before it reached its destination, sending a brief flow of water onto the sand and then tuck itself under the new wave and timidly return to sea as though exhausted and defeated - it had been beaten by another. It seemed so ironic and yet beautiful that it happened over and over, just as it had for thousands of years. He wondered how many waves had tried to reach this very shore where he stood; how many times had someone stood here and asked that question. The sand looked so clean and untouched that it was hard to believe that anyone had ever been here before.

Sam began a survey of his surroundings. He felt the hard smooth wood beneath him and considered where it may have come from – part of a shipwreck from some long ago storm or battle – or maybe just a part of a fallen tree that had been captured by the sea. Its shapeless form left little evidence. Rising up from the sand, it appeared to be only a small portion of something much larger. Sam ran his hand along the smooth surface and marveled at how time and the sea had 'sanded' it smoother than wood he had finished in the shop at home. Moving farther up the 'log' he settled on the end, letting his feet dangle freely like he had as a boy on a teeter-totter. From his perch on the driftwood log, he could look at waves coming in from far away – rising, falling and building up again sometimes to break with a white spray, a distance away; sometimes rolling, building into mounds that moved ever closer and closer to the shore. The sky was a bright blue all the way to the horizon where it met the sparkling dark green-blue of the sea. Only the bright sun broke the canopy as it stretched all around him without a cloud in sight.

Sam took stock of his surroundings. It was mid-morning and he had no idea how far he had walked. Focusing only on his footsteps, he had not realized how far those footsteps had taken him. Now, the only company he had was the gulls who flew in and out over the water, searching, diving, and crying out to one another. He watched and marveled as they climbed, faced the wind where they then seemed to hang motionless between heaven and earth. Time seemed to stop for a moment as they moved neither forward nor back. Time stopped for Sam too. He could no longer see the cottage. He could only see the beach to the left and right, stretching out in both directions. The strange sensation added to his moment of solitude. There were rocks and crannies in places reaching out into the ocean. He hadn't noticed them before. His tracks disappeared to the left into wave-washed sand. He knew that he had to retrace those steps and return to the cottage to settle and plan his day, but somehow it didn't seem as important as he thought it should. He had neither time-clock nor agenda to meet. He had no deadlines or appointments. He had no one to answer to. He felt suddenly both free and alone. He rose from his perch and to his feet and started back the way he had come.

The trip back seemed a lot longer than Sam remembered it as he had walked the other way. As he retraced his path back to the cottage, he noticed more than he had previously. There were little inlets and rocks and occasional bits of debris that he must have stepped over before. He had been so lost in his thoughts that he hadn't seen anything. Now he began to take notice: On one side, the ocean; on the other side, sandy dunes rising – some gradually and some quite steeply to small hills of sand. Now he noticed, too, that he was not entirely alone. An islander was in sight in a boat out a way from the beach. As he passed a break in the dunes, he thought he caught sight of a distant village. He hadn't even noticed anything on his way down the beach this morning; now he saw signs of life. He climbed a high dune for a better view and then another to see the village. It was some distance away from the beach, nestled in a large grove of trees. From his vantage point he could look down into the panorama of native life unnoticed, as he had so many times as a kid, watched an ant hill or a bee hive.

It was a cluster of very small square buildings, all basically alike – no windows, only open doors and 'lawns' of sand. In front of each house was a fire pit and a bench or two. Hammocks were hung here and there between trees. There didn't seem to be any streets in the village – just these 'houses' scattered as though they had been tossed into place on each side of one wide 'path – thirty or more of them, each looking just like the other. They were built of vertical poles, probably bamboo, he thought, and roofed with either thatch or corrugated tin. At the far end of this 'main path' was a larger building, with a crude cross attached to the top of its gabled roof. At the near end of the path on one side, several small wooden canoes were parked and on the other side of the path was what appeared to be a tiny 'store' – nothing more than an open fronted building with a counter across it. The little store seemed to be the center of some noisy activity. The small village was like a busy beehive. Women were busily doing chores about their homes. Children played in the yards. He could smell the aroma of burning firewood.

Sam looked at the tiny gardens surrounding the village. Suddenly he remembered the huge garden of his mother. He envisioned the neatly spaced rows of vegetables that she had meticulously weeded and cared for. He remembered the tomato plants that she prided in – tall stakes holding them up ("never let a tomato touch the ground", she would say.)... the peppers, and cabbages had their place next to the tomatoes and then rows and rows of carrots, beets, radishes, beans and peas….and the sprawling cucumber and squash plants.

Mother had been very proud of her garden. It supplied the family year round – first from the fresh picking in summer and then canning for winter. The cans were all stored in rows in the basement on the old wooden shelves that Dad had built for her when they married and she first moved to the farm. Mom had taken to farm life even though she had come from a different sort. She seemed to enjoy the hard work that surrounded the daily chores and responsibilities. He could see her in his mind's eye, her apron fluttering when she would run to the chicken house for just one egg that she needed for a recipe or her straw hat as she knelt in the garden, toiling over her precious plants. She would have liked this scene where the natives tended their gardens as a part of their daily chores and a part of their provision.

As Sam recounted the garden, his mind wandered to the fields of home as well. He could almost hear the corn rustling in the wind in summer and the different rustling as it was cut and carried in, in the fall. He recalled fondly, the wheat in the open wagon as it flowed from the combine auger and how, as a boy, he had climbed into the wagon barefoot and felt the cool grain just as he felt the sand beneath his feet now. He recounted how he had started at an early age to do the work of a man while he was yet a boy and that barefoot feeling had lingered even though he soon was on the tractor, doing the same work as a grown-up.

"That is why I needed this time away", he thought… "I never had a chance to decide to grow up and be a man, it just happened. And now I am responsible for it all! Am I really ready?" "I am a lot like these people – life is just thrust at them, no choice, just expected to follow the same rituals and routines as their ancestors."

He had heard it once, in church – that 'you had to WANT to live the good life…' But he wasn't sure he really knew what the 'good life' was or what life he did want to live.

"Do I want to be forced to live a life that is not really my desire?" He questioned. "Do I want to be what I am expected to be?"

As he turned back to the beach, he realized that there was a wooden boat on the shore. Surely he should have seen that this morning, but maybe they had just come in from a night of fishing. There was another boat in the water about a half-mile out from shore. He couldn't make out whether it was a fisherman, but reckoned it must be. Turning again to his homeward path, he saw the figure of someone on a small dune, sleeping on a blanket, a towel covering head and shoulders as if to block out the sun. He wondered briefly who it might be and why they were there, and if people here slept on the beach often and how he had missed seeing this sleeper when he started out. He wondered if they had even been there. He dismissed it and continued toward his cottage. Finally it came into sight and he turned to climb the crunchy shell path and then the steps to his porch.

He stopped and turned to look back. His cottage was situated neatly in a secluded spot between two large dunes that nearly hid him from the rest of the world. He knew that the town was only a short distance away, and the village that he had passed was also only a half mile or so in the other direction, but his only view was of the sea, the sand, and behind the cottage, the overgrowth of foliage. It was a peaceful spot. He felt a little uneasy for some reason, but completely confident that he had made the right decision and was right where he wanted to be. His head was filled with thoughts of memories - and now questions about his new surroundings. He walked into the cottage and flopped down on the rickety old bed.

Chapter 3

Sam opened his eyes and realized that he had been sleeping. He looked at his watch. It was 4:00! That walk had taken a lot out of him. He smiled sheepishly to himself. He would never have fallen asleep like that in the middle of the day back home. Hunger soon reminded Sam that he hadn't eaten anything since he landed on this island. He had been so tired yesterday when he arrived at the cottage that he had laid down and gone right to sleep. This morning, he had left before breakfast and then fallen asleep when he got home. Now, he needed something to eat. He looked around, wondering what direction to go for groceries, and noticed that there was a big basket of fruit on a small table in the corner – was that there when he arrived? "I guess so", he answered his own thoughts as he tore off a banana and settled into a chair. Tomorrow would be soon enough to go grocery shopping.

Sam surveyed the cottage again and took stock of his accommodations, making a mental list of things he would need. He hadn't brought anything but a few changes of clothes and the personal necessities.

He would have to buy a few things soon. He looked in the refrigerator and found it nearly empty. In the cupboards, there were a few dishes – pots and pans; he figured he would be amply outfitted for anything he might want to cook or serve to himself. He hadn't thought about how long he would be staying, but decided that it would be a pretty easy lifestyle from the looks of things. Pulling another banana from the bowl of fruit, he headed out to the porch.

"Ahhhhhhhhhh, what a life . . .!"

he said to himself aloud as he settled gingerly into the hammock that was strung across the end of the porch. The ropes creaked and the hammock sagged a little, but held and he wiggled to adjust to the middle of it. He could hear the mixed sounds around him in the distance - the waves repeating their rhythm, and the cries of the gulls coming from different directions. The sounds seemed to blend together, making a symphony of peace. The sun was getting low over the water and he decided to tune in to the sounds and wait for the sunset.

The bright blue sky of the day had changed to a lighter blue as the sun seemed to become brighter in a different way. Suddenly, colors seemed to come from nowhere – gold and yellow and orange - the sky became vivid with color – colors like he had never seen. He watched them change from the yellow-white glow around the sun burning against a blue sky to streaks of orange against a paler blue and then from orange to red as it settled slowly to the horizon and reflected on the water – reflected a path of red patches atop each wave like wobbly stepping stones from the beach to the horizon. The sun settled slowly and then, in an almost visible movement, it sank quickly into the sea, leaving behind a panorama of red and orange and grey-blue. The birds crossed to and fro like silhouettes against the colored sky as though in a dance to celebrate the ending of the day. He knew they would soon be in search of a resting place to wait for the morrow to begin the cycle again. Sam stretched out in his hammock; drinking it all in until the last streak of red had faded to grey and the night sky crept down to the sea to follow the sun. A cool breeze came in from the water and stars began to blink into sight. Sam shivered a little as a breeze swirled around him, but he didn't want to move. He shifted a little in the hammock and watched the stars against the now black sky – It was a sky quite like the summer sky over the wheat fields of Iowa, but the air gave a feeling strangely different. It was so peaceful and quiet that he felt totally alone. He pulled the blanket that was rolled up at his feet over him and lay absorbed in the night that surrounded him.

Chapter 4

It was morning. Sam hardly remembered climbing out of the hammock and into his bed last night; but now sunlight streamed in through the open door and windows, greeting him with a late start to a new day. Sam showered, shaved, and combed his shock of brown hair, pulled on some jeans and a polo shirt, and slipped his feet into his sandals, surveyed what he saw in the mirror and reckoned he was "ready for town".

Descending the steps and the path from the cottage to the road, he felt a little uneasy about leaving the sanctuary of his hide-out and actually facing whatever may confront him in town, but remembering the empty cupboards, he decided that it was time. He walked the road, trying to remember what he had seen in the taxi ride out two days ago. The sandy road was firm beneath his feet, but seemed more of a trail than a road. He remembered that it widened somewhere and was paved, but here it was barely different from the sand on either side. He passed through the walls of brush that he had remembered, on a carpet of the tiny leaves, green, yellow and brown that had fallen from the overhanging branches; and then out into the open again as the road passed closer to the beach. Some places he was quite close to the water and other times the beach reached out into the sea with sand bars or rocky reaches. The distance to town seemed much longer than it had in the taxi. The dunes on the other side of the road were alternately bare knolls or covered with waving grasses and low shrub that seemed to somehow defy the winds and salt air. Beyond, he could see small hills in the distance and, far away, the mound of the mountain that he suspected was, or had been, a volcano. He wondered how many miles away it was – maybe five or so? It seemed to just protrude harmlessly from the relatively low hills around it. There were tall palm trees with coconuts visible under their fronds, and short, fat palms that seemed to have no fruit. There were some kind of leafy trees that resembled oaks, and climbing vines and flowers – flowers everywhere – tiny ones close to the sand and large ones on vines and in small clumps in the shade of the trees. Ahead, he saw houses on the island side of the road - small houses with sandy yards and shrubs around them. The houses seemed to be built of rough boards on stilts above the sand, much like the cottage he lived in. They had the same porches and tin roofs. He wondered if they, too, were rentals. How many people came here like he did, to stay for a brief escape from the world in these old primitive beach houses? The road widened suddenly to a paved surface of some kind of mixture of shells and coral and concrete. It was a chalky grey and a little dusty underfoot. There was no sidewalk, just the street and the sandy shoulder on either side. This must be the 'city limits', he thought to himself as he began to see a different scene. The houses looked more substantial and now lined both sides of the street. Their yards extended to the shoulder, most with a sort of grassy lawn, and trees shading the house and yard. Some were small and cottage looking, but on a foundation rather than the stilts that his was built on. All seemed to have the same tin roof, but some were steeper pitched and some were painted.

Some of the houses were painted brightly, some had a pale whitewash look; but all of the houses and lawns seemed well cared for and attractive – every window had shutters. Each house had a welcoming look with a path of stones or crushed shells leading to the door. There was little activity apparent in the street or about the houses. Here and there, a resident would be sweeping their stoop or tending a garden. Each would stop as he passed and nod or wave to him with a smile as if to say hello. Side streets stretched past the houses toward the beach and a block or two in the other direction on the island side of the street. He could see other houses similar to the ones on the main street. Closer to the business area, some of the houses were larger, but all seemed to have the same basic look. Some had little fences around their yards; and here and there, reminders of the sea – a huge ship's wheel hung from a standard with the name "Capt. Smith" on a placard across the center… an ancient anchor leaned against a flagpole in another yard…remnants of ship parts were used as décor over doorways and porches… half a huge killer clam shell filled with flowers in the center of another yard…there were flowers everywhere. Palm trees became more and more prevalent and shade trees seemed to be larger closer to the business district.

The business district seemed to be only a dozen or so shops on the main street and most of it was houses that had been converted to shops or were still houses with a small shop occupying the front of the house. The shops were all open – literally 'open' - with the wares on display outside, in doorways, and inside, on shelves or tables or hanging from the ceiling. At a quick glance, Sam could see that the shops were very small and close together, many selling the same kind of wares. There were fruit stands with all kinds of produce, souvenir shops, clothing shops, jewelry shops and a larger building that looked like it had been built to actually be a store. It had 'General Store' on the sign overhead and outside stood a barrel with brooms sticking out of it. Intermixed with the shops was a building with a restaurant sign over the door and another with the expected 'bar' sign. Across the street another bar and another restaurant marked 'Café'. There were a few people on the street looking at merchandise but Sam wondered if there were enough people to support the shops. Near the end of the line of shops loomed the hotel that Sam had seen before. It didn't seem so impressive today – a taxi stood under the portico in the half-circle drive and there were a couple of people beside it with suitcases. The taxi was the only motorized vehicle he saw, but there were a few bicycles in sight.

Sam decided to visit each shop and explore the town before picking up his staples and going 'home' – or perhaps make it a day and see what the night life would bring.

The first shop was a clothing shop that had taken over the front part of a house. Sam didn't expect to buy anything, but wanted to explore. It appeared to be a rather exclusive shop – not the usual tourist place, but he found that inside it did have jeans and shirts – along with some more dressy clothes and at one side, some very frilly dresses and skirts and blouses. An attractive, well-dressed older lady greeted Sam almost as soon as he entered the door. She spoke with a genteel voice and asked if she could show him anything.

He stuttered an answer of 'Just browsing", to which she offered a wave of the hand to indicate that the store was at his disposal, then offered a cup of tea, motioning to a chair at a small table near a window. He was tired and warm. The shop seemed refreshingly cool and her invitation was too nice to refuse. He moved toward the chair and she hurried to pour tea from a china teapot into two small china cups on saucers. She sat and he followed. She began a conversation by introducing herself as Antoinetta and her accent confirmed that she was of French background. Her pale blue eyes sparkled with excitement as she started to tell of her shop before he could introduce himself.

"I offer the best in clothing for men and women", she cheerfully added. "many of the native women like the frilly dresses for Sundays and celebrations. They can't afford much, so I try to sell them as cheaply as I can. They are not as expensive as they look." She smiled an embarrassed smile as though she had just realized that she was rambling and interrupted herself with, "Are you on the island for long?"

Sam had been studying her more than listening – she was thin, attractive, had nearly snow white hair pulled up into some kind of roll at the back of her head, with a few wisps encircling her face, - a face accented by an infectious, bright smile of nearly perfect white teeth. She wore little make-up, but had a faint redness of lipstick and a bit of blush on her cheeks. Suddenly hearing the question, he responded that he 'really wasn't sure yet'.

"You are staying in the Marshall place aren't you?, she asked.

Taken aback by her being so well informed, he paused for a moment then nodded and offered his, "I'm Sam – Samuel Malone. I came here for a sort of open-ended visit."

She seemed satisfied and began her own story again, explaining that she was the widow of the late Captain Duval. He had shipwrecked in a typhoon several years ago and she couldn't bring herself to leave him.

"I got a little from his insurance and decided to build this shop in our home to support myself. I like it here and have met some lovely people. I hope you will enjoy your stay and find whatever you are looking for, Sam."

She stood, as though signaling an end to the conversation. Sam took the cue and rose to leave. He thanked her for the tea and turned toward the door.

"Good-bye, please come again!" she called after him as he stepped back out into the sunlight.

Sam turned to survey the shops before him one after another. In the next small open shop, a young, blonde, dark-skinned girl in a long, loose, flowered dress sat on a stool, idly braiding what looked like strands of sea grass into a bracelet. Perhaps it was the tall stool, or the length of the dress that followed her shapely body and almost covered her bare feet, but she looked tall and thin. She didn't move or interrupt her task, but greeted Sam with a silent smile as he poked through her display of island jewelry made of grasses, cords, shells, bits of colored glass and coral. Her eyes followed Sam with a curious questioning look, but she said nothing until he began to leave; and then she, as though to an old friend, said a cheery "Bye for now!"

Sam, now intrigued by the first two shops, took the few steps toward the third. Suddenly he stopped, transfixed by a display in front of this shop. A large panel of vertical bamboo poles was the support for several paintings... scenes of the island and portraits of children. One painting in particular caught his eye – it appeared to be the very cottage he lived in! The paintings were unframed – some on stretched canvas, but others on driftwood and shells and other backgrounds. He leaned closer to inspect the work and wondered at the artist. The only clue was a small K in the corner of each painting. He stood for a long time admiring the work and the mood that it apparently carried. Some of the paintings were so gay and light, while others seemed sad and somber. Each mood was intense, as though the very voice of the artist was speaking out from the canvas. There was a painting of an old man – brown-skinned with white hair. The wrinkles on his face seemed so real that Sam wanted to reach out and touch them to reassure himself that it was only a painting. A tiny shell adorned with a painted flower made Sam bend to smell for the aroma he thought might be there. His eyes traveled over the paintings again and again – not wanting to miss any, he was tempted to buy one but forced himself to move on.

"What other surprises will I find?" he wondered as he struggled to leave the paintings. As he stepped around the painting display, he found it to be part of a shop of seashells, glass floats, and driftwood – odd shaped bits of things that the sea had given up and now were here for sale. He wondered who on the island would buy what they might find for themselves anywhere along the beaches. He stepped into the shop to find carvings of birds and fish made from the same bits of driftwood; and behind a small table, the carver at work. He was a small, dark man with a shiny bald head, glasses on the end of his nose and a small knife in his hand laboring over his craft.

He barely looked up, but continuing at his task, greeted Sam with a sturdy "Hello! You are welcome to look around. Tell me if you want anything."

Sam noted that there was little room to move around or even to stand, but he could see many hours of labor in every corner. It was apparent that there was artistic talent on this island. He wondered, but didn't ask, if this wood carver was also the painter, of if he was selling them for someone else.

Back in the sunlight, Sam realized that he was not alone in his tour. There were now several others, obviously tourists, browsing the shops – each examining the displays along the street and politely taking turns entering the small shops. They nodded to Sam as they crossed paths.

Sam stopped at the produce shop and inspected the fruit. He didn't recognize some of the things, but vowed to learn each one. He decided to come back later for the things he wanted to take to the cottage. A round little man with a huge moustache and a straw hat welcomed him to 'inspect and make a good choice!' He said, "See you soon!" as Sam left; and Sam replied that he would be back. The little man beamed and turned toward another customer.

Next to the produce shop, was another shop of food – with a sign boasting 'RARE AND EXOTIC FOODS' it was barely more than a huge pantry, with doors swung open wide like the doors of a kitchen cupboard, and shelves on both doors, there were spices, herbs, and elixirs of all kinds, with some of the more recognizable to Sam – pop tarts and Hershey bars joined several varieties of cereals, teas, and syrups from several countries. A bright red and white awning over the top, gave it the feel of a county fair. Sam was too curious to pass this one up, so stopped to investigate. The owner was a jolly, plump lady who said her husband traveled a lot and acquired a taste for many different foods in his travels.

"He always brought me samples of things – sometimes whole cases. So I decided to share them with the islanders." she said. Some of the natives have come to sample foods from other lands, but mostly tourists are intrigued by them - or look for something that reminds them of home. Since I started the store, I have had requests, so send out for some of the items that sell well."

Sam bought a box of his favorite frosted flakes and tucked the box under his arm and proceeded on down the street.

As he passed the bar, he looked inside the open door to see a long wooden bar with crude wooden stools, small round tables and chairs on an old wooden floor. There were the sounds of laughter and echoing chatter coming from the dimly lit room that made it sound quite inviting. The overhead fans turning slowly looked almost hypnotic and Sam imagined that many an hour could be spent here escaping the heat. He wondered if this was the place his Marine buddies had spoken of.

Realizing that he had a box of cereal under his arm, Sam welcomed the shop next to the bar which had beach towels, hand-painted t-shirts, and totes. There were canvas bags – 'just right for shopping', he thought. He passed up the flowered ones and selected a sensible sturdy bag with a rope handle, paid for it, and stuffed his box of cereal into it as he left.

The restaurant next door, looked almost modern and American – small, but accommodating. In the window of the door, was an 'OPEN' sign and a small menu with the 'special of the day' on a note attached with a paper clip. Sam stopped to read the menu and noticed that although fish seemed to be the main offering, 'country fried chicken' and steak were also available – a little more costly. Glancing through the window, Sam could see that the restaurant was already busy.

The next store seemed a little more substantial –
as though it had been one of the first buildings built
for that purpose - and many years ago. It was a
grocery store, sporting regular counters and shelves
of canned and boxed foods. Sam entered, ready to
buy a few things. He scanned the shelves and found
canned vegetables and soups, the usual bags and
boxes of flour, sugar, rice, and beans. Behind the
counter, a dark boy of 16 or so offered to help Sam
if he needed to find something, and from the back
of the store, appeared a friendly bearded man in his
middle forties to echo the offer.

Bob Andrews extended his hand and introduced
himself with a smile to welcome Sam to the store and
'full service'. Sam thanked them both but declined
the offer, choosing to browse on his own. Bob
followed him down the aisle asking if he was the new
tenant in the Marshall place. Sam confirmed that he
was and introduced himself as Sam Malone. They
chatted for a moment as Sam selected some items and
placed them on the counter, carefully making sure
he didn't get more than he could carry home. Bob
noticed what he was doing and offered to deliver the
groceries if Sam wanted him to. Sam said he would

let him know. Realizing that he didn't want to carry it around town, he asked if he could leave his purchases and come back for them. Bob agreed. Sam finished, paid, and left, promising to return in an hour or so.

Stepping out of Bob Andrews' grocery, Sam noted that he had covered most of the shops in town! There was, of course, the other side of the street, so maybe he was half-way. Next door to the grocery was the General store. It was, like the grocery store, a substantial building, obviously built a long time ago and just for this purpose. It stood like a monument to a by-gone era, with its wooden steps leading into a central door, windows on either side displaying all the items one could imagine – some like museum pieces, and some like they had been transported from a modern discount department store in America. There were lanterns and flashlights, fishing equipment and knives, tools and silverware… Drawn in by this tantalizing array, Sam found a shopper's paradise. He imagined that some of the things hanging on hooks from the ceiling had been there since the store first opened; and in the showcases even more of the same – some dust-covered, some shiny new looking. There were bins of nails and various hardware items, as well as plumbing and electrical supplies – and across the room, larger bins of clothing, such as shorts and jeans and shirts. A huge pair of overalls hung on the wall above as though waiting for a giant to need them. A little sign dangled from one leg saying "It these fit you, they are free". Sam chuckled at the joke and went deeper into the large room. In the back, some grocery items were on shelves behind a counter and Sam wondered how many would come grocery shopping here with the grocery next door. He wondered how long some of the items had been on those dusty shelves.

Sam was met by a sturdily built man in his mid-forties, slightly balding, wearing a denim apron over denim shorts and a grey T-shirt. He was busily working - 'stocking' - carrying a box of small items to some appropriate shelves or bins someplace. He nodded and said a short, "'Lo" to Sam as they passed. Sam was left to his explorations. There was suntan lotion, toiletries, fishing hooks, machetes, sandals, boots, hats, belts, gloves, and writing supplies…. Sam imagined that anything anyone could ever need on this island, could be purchased here… and Sam was pretty sure if he asked that guy with the apron, he would know right where to look for it.

As he turned to leave, Sam noticed a small partitioned-off area with a caged window and a sign over the window that said "mail". Sam realized that the general store was also the post office and suspected that no one delivered the mail, but rather it was picked up here by the residents.

Suddenly, an attractive, middle-aged woman with short cropped hair and a long, flowing, flowered dress came from apparent nowhere and apologized for not meeting Sam at the door.

"I was in the back room and didn't hear you come in." She said. "Are you looking for something in particular? We have most everything, but sometimes it is hard to find things if you don't know your way around." she smiled. "I am Florence, they all call me Flo, and that is Ben, my husband over there. We try to help you find the impossible…"

Sam watched her blue eyes look him over and realized that she, like everyone in town, probably was more interested in who he was and why he was here than in him as a customer. She had a quick, closed-mouth smile, that seemed to form naturally, exposing a pleasantness about her that was easy to respond to. He noted a hint of a southern accent in her speech and wondered where she may have originated from and how long she may have been here.

"No, not really." He replied, and introduced himself and added, "I am just getting the lay of the land. You have a really intriguing store! I think I could spend hours in here, just looking."

Her smile broadened to reveal shiny white teeth and merry dimples in her cheeks. "Well, let me show you around, by all means!" She offered with a sweeping wave, and led him from counter to counter and bin to bin, pointing out the areas that were obvious, and a few that were less obvious – explaining each one. They passed her husband who never looked up from his stocking chores as she chattered on with "I know you may not be looking to buy anything just now, but at least you will know where it is." She smiled her dimpled smile again as they finished the circle and returned to the front of the store. She confirmed Sam's suspicions about the post office and added,

"Someone is usually around here til' close to dark".

She extended a hand as though to take his and he took it in a polite handshake.

"Thank you for your hospitality. You have been very nice." Sam said as he left.

An ancient public phone booth stood next to the general store and it suddenly occurred to Sam that he had not had contact with the outside world and wondered for a moment if he should try to call someone. He decided against it.

There was a wide green area like a park between the general store and the hotel setting the building off as though it were the town's greatest attraction. The hotel was an older building but well constructed and perfectly maintained. It had been built in the style of a southern plantation home. The drive circled under a portico in the front with steps leading up to a grand entrance on a wide veranda. Brightly colored chairs lined the veranda, standing in sharp contrast to the gleaming white of the building. Sam could see through the wide open door, a large lobby and a sweeping stairway leading to the upper floors. Sam felt a little alienated from the hotel because he was not a part of that activity, but he stopped at the entrance to the park area and took in the view of all that it offered. It was from here that the tourists trickled into the shops. It was here that they returned with their purchases and it was here that they seemed to find security. For those in the hotel, it seemed to be their world. There were walks through the lawns and gardens of flowers. There were benches and outdoor lounge chairs. The area was filled with flower gardens and shade trees intermixed with palms. Sam expected a pool, but the wide gardens extended to a beautiful beach area on a natural cove quite sheltered by surrounding low palms and other plants. A row of lounge chairs sat across the beach as an invitation to guests. He envisioned dozens of guests mixing, talking, relaxing together like a human beehive. He saw only a few – here and there, more alone than mixing...

Sam realized that this had been a morning of distraction. He had not spent one moment in thought of his own problems! He had been so busy in his explorations that all of that had been for the moment forgotten. He was like a kid playing hooky from school, but he knew he would have to return to those thoughts. The treasures here were not what he was seeking. His quest was entirely different, and he would have to confront the issues that had brought him to Pangatango and to this very moment. But he would think about that later.

Shaking off the thoughts and crossing the street, Sam passed a small barber shop. It was a tiny square building with a large window giving view to the inside where there were two chairs and little else. He only saw one chair in use, and wondered if there was more than one barber. The 'waiting room' seemed to be outside, for under a crudely painted barber pole was a bench with two occupants apparently not in a hurry to get inside, and on the others side of the door was an ancient wooden rocker, also occupied. The three men seemed quite content in their conversation. Perhaps they were not even waiting for the barber, but were just resting. Sam wondered if anything or anyone ever hurried on this island. The barber shop stood alone not far from the fence that surrounded the airport. The fence extended back for some distance and along the street for several blocks toward the airport terminal that he remembered from his arrival.

Next door to the barber shop was another small block building with the word 'BANK' in large letters across the front above the door and window. As Sam looked down the street, he was reminded of an old western town scene and almost expected to see cowboys ride up with bandanas over their faces, guns drawn and announce that they were robbing the bank… He would come back to the bank another time.

Sam stood for a moment looking at the quaint scene. He looked back at the shops he had entered. He considered each business and each person. He looked to the shops he had not visited and wondered if there was anything new to discover. There was, of course, the bank that he should visit, and the barber shop, and another bar and next to it the café and a few more of the tourist shops that might hold some interesting surprises. There was also a used shop which Sam suspected meant 'junk' shop. He suspected that he might find it interesting if he explored it…

As he stood in thought, the sky overhead suddenly darkened. Obscured by clouds, the blue sky turned to an ominous grey. The street suddenly came alive with activity. Sam watched in wonder as Shopkeepers rushed to 'close up'. They hurriedly took their wares inside or covered them with brightly colored plastic sheets. The blonde carried her jewelry trays and hanging racks inside. The unique exotic food lady closed the doors of her displayed shelves. The wood carver left his shop only long enough to carefully cover the paintings with a large plastic tarp. Antonetta stood on her front porch watching as though to give her dignified approval to the proceedings.

Suddenly, as though on some silent signal, it began to rain – not a growing rain from a little sprinkle, but just like a shower had been turned on, it came straight down. Sam ran for shelter like all the rest. He hurried into the nearby café and stood uncertainly in the doorway.

"Welcome to Pangatango!" A laughing young lady greeted him, "Come in and sit down. It won't last long."

Sam moved to a table near the door, and sat down, wiping the water from his face, and looked up at the smiling face still there as though waiting for a response.

Sam laughed out loud and said, "You sure know how to bring in the customers!"

She returned his laugh with one of her own and, "Well, now that you are here…." She handed him a cardboard menu and disappeared into the kitchen, then returned with a glass of water before Sam barely had a chance to settle.

"I'll need a minute." He said, but she hovered nearby straightening up chairs and the accessories on the empty tables around him.

Sam decided that he was hungry and maybe food did sound good.

"How about breakfast?" he ventured, and she hurried back to his side. She stood close enough that her body touched his shoulder and he moved instinctively away but she didn't notice.

"Ok, my name is Mara" she said "... and you certainly can have breakfast if you like!"

He pointed to the omelet on the menu as she looked over his shoulder.

"And coffee would be nice." he added.

Mara scribbled something on her pad and hurried off, her long black pony tail bouncing.

Sam watched her walk away – a small, but well built girl with curves in all the right places.

A moment later, she was back and settled into the chair across from Sam at his table!

"It has been a busy morning..." she began, "I have been on my feet all morning, do you mind if I sit?"

He shrugged a 'no problem' reply as she settled into the chair.

She leaned toward Sam, as though to start a conversation, but resting her ample bosom on the table and her chin in her hands she closed her eyes as though in exhaustion. Her hands were unadorned – no rings or nail polish – the hands of a working girl. Her face carried faint lines of maturity, but he thought her to be still quite young. She slowly opened her dark brown eyes and wearily started, "The rain comes like that often…" she explained, then regaining her earlier sparkle, she broke into a smile and added "…and when it comes, you better be ready or you get wet!" She straightened in her chair laughing again and eyed Sam quizzically.

"I am new here." He began, "I guess I have a lot to learn."

They both laughed. He really didn't want to make small talk, and Mara didn't seem to mind his reluctance to speak; she sat quietly with her hands clasped on the table in front of her, apparently just content with a moment of rest. The rest of the café was empty except for one person in the far back corner.

Mara followed Sam's gaze and quickly explained, "That's 'Gimmie' – he calls himself Jimmy, but he is always looking for handouts so most folks call him Gimmie. He don't mind. He don't talk much. Nobody really knows who he is or where he came from or where he lives. He just shows up now and then. We give him leftovers if he carries out the trash or sweeps up a little."

Gimmie looked as though he had never shaved or had a haircut, but maybe had hacked some of his hair off by himself now and then. His hair was matted and stood out like a picture Sam had once seen of a bushman in the National Geographic. His whiskers covered most of his face so it was hard to discern any features, but he had a far-away look in his eyes as he seemed to stare right through Sam. Sam looked away, but the image stayed in his mind as he turned back to Mara, who was quietly watching.

As though on cue, the silence was broken by a sharp voice from the kitchen and Mara jumped to her feet with a "Back to work..." over her shoulder and rushed off to get Sam's meal. Gimmie shuffled past Sam and out the door. Sam watched him through the window as he ambled into the street in worn sandals and old baggy army fatigues. He carried a knapsack that was held together with rope – maybe his only possessions. Gimmie stopped in the middle of the street, in the rain, as though lost, then regaining his direction, crossed the street and stood aimlessly in the shelter of the red and white awning of the exotic food place. Sam wondered about him for a moment, but his thoughts were interrupted by the return of Mara and his meal.

She smiled and said, "Enjoy!" and hurried off to clean the table that Gimmie had left.

By the time Sam had finished his meal, the rain had stopped. He watched through the window as he sat for a moment, collecting his thoughts. He watched the street come back to life and Gimmie shuffle out of sight. The shops reopened and the sun reappeared.

Mara was back by his side; hovering close again. "I hope you enjoyed your breakfast. Will that be all?" She pressed. It was apparent that she was in no hurry for him to leave, but would rather have someone to talk to.

Sam shrugged a silent end to the meal and the conversation. He handed her a bill and watched her bounce away for change. Something inside him stirred at the movement of her body and the cheerful company she had been, but he had other things on his mind. He rose to go, leaving a generous tip from the change she brought. She noticed and thanked him profusely asking him to come back soon. He nodded, smiled, and said a polite good-bye.

Back in the street, Sam continued his exploration, shop by shop. – a quiet little jewelry store of more island jewelry as well as some substantial pieces of rings, bracelets, watches and necklaces that were obviously not island made. From the jewelry store, he continued to another shop of clothing – simple blouses and dresses as well as shirts and shorts for both men and women. The clothing hung on portable racks that were both inside and outside of the small building. The store was watched over by a young woman who seemed little interested in Sam or anyone else who ventured in. She stood near the back of the store idly fingering her bracelet and staring off into space. Sam offered a smile, but she didn't seem to notice. Sam moved on to the next store.

The next shop was an old house with its door wide open and a sign on a pole leaning against the door jamb. The sign read "Antiques" but inside it looked more like a collection of items that had been cast off from everywhere. It appeared that someone lived in the midst of all of the collection and just allowed folk to wander through. Curiosity got the best of Sam and he began examining the 'antiques'. There were several rooms of tools, shoes, pots and pans, some pieces of furniture, and glass cases of jewelry, keys, coins and silverware. One shelf held a few well-worn toys and another, some old yellowed books. A couple doors were closed – to the living rooms of the owner, Sam assumed. In the middle of the largest room, at a scarred old table, sat a thin, balding man with wire-rimmed glasses, busily calculating figures on an ancient adding machine. There was a pile of papers on the table and long strips of adding machine tape curled up in a pile. He looked over his glasses at Sam for a moment and returned to his numbers. Sam found an old war pistol and wondered about its origin, but laid it back down carefully and left the shop.

"Well, that is it for town." Sam said aloud to himself as he stepped back into the sunlight. He glanced up and down the street as though he hoped to find more, but resigned himself to the reality of his situation. He started back toward the grocery and his purchases when he noticed a young lady at the display of art that he had admired earlier. She seemed to be adding something to the display, and had her back to him and his curiosity drew him to return to the shop. By the time he got there, she was gone. He searched for a change in the display, but noticed nothing.

"Was she the artist? – or just a browsing customer? Why was he so curious?" He wondered as he walked back to Bob Andrew's store.

Bob was waiting for him when he arrived."How do you like our town?" he asked.

"It is all I could have imagined." Sam replied.

"What shall we do with your groceries?"

Sam looked at the boxes and at his small tote bag and they both laughed.

"I guess I will need that help, Bob!" he stammered.

And with a twinkle in his eye, Bob assured him that 'something could be arranged...'

Sam wanted to stay and chat. He wanted to ask about Gimmie, He wanted to ask about the old antiques, and about the whole town and how it had come to be. He wanted to ask about the artist who was only a K on canvas, but had captured his curiosity. He felt comfortable with Bob and knew they were going to be friends, but dismissed the questions for now with a "Thank you".

"I can give you a lift with your groceries." Bob offered,

Sam said there was no hurry with the groceries and that he really wanted to walk. Bob promised the delivery 'before dark'. They shook hands and Sam started back down the street. He stopped at the fruit stand and picked up a nice bunch of bananas, which fit nicely into his tote and studied a small round reddish-orange fruit for a moment. The man with the mustache explained that it was a mango and explained how to eat it. Sam added one to his tote and headed for 'home'. His mind was now filled with new thoughts of all he had seen and heard. His own problems seemed to be less important for a while.

Chapter 5

The morning broke bright and sunny as usual. Sam was out of bed and onto the beach to greet the sunrise. He walked the short distance to the water and scanned the horizon for any sign of life. He felt unusually alone this morning and even the glimpse of a boat might cheer him. He knew that on the other side of the dunes, lay a whole village of people… and in the opposite direction down the road was the town with friendly faces - and perhaps a chat with Bob…

It had been days since his trip to town and he wasn't really anxious to return. Sam didn't want to look for people. He didn't want to chat. He just didn't like this empty feeling that seemed to overwhelm him night and day. He strolled back to the safety of his porch and settled into the hammock. He could still look out over the ocean into an empty horizon. He could still hear the lapping of the waves. He could still watch the gulls…. But he was alone. He closed his eyes as if to shut out the world but it seemed even more intense. He tried to push away the thoughts of home and unanswered questions, but they pounded at his brain. He tried to focus on one thought at a time but they all rushed at him at once. Sam drifted into a soothing nap.

Mid-morning, Sam woke with a start. He had been dreaming. He couldn't remember what the dream was about, but he knew it disturbed him – not like a nightmare, but like a troubling riddle… if only he could remember…

Sam spoke aloud as he entered the house, picked up a water bottle, and a piece of fruit. . .

"I will walk it off."

He headed down the beach that he had walked every day since his arrival. "I will walk until I can clear my head!" he promised himself.

Sam wandered inland a little and climbed the dunes, hoping to see something new as he crested each one. In the distance, lay the mountain, ever teasing him, beckoning him.

"What is it about that mountain?" he mused. Atop the next dune, again, "What is it about that mountain?" He returned to the beach and settled onto a log half buried in the sand, looking back at his tracks in the sand. Then he noticed another set of tracks. Someone had passed while he was on the dune. Sam had never been a hunter, but he had learned to observe, and he noticed that this set of footprints was much smaller than his. The person was a small person, - "a child? No, bigger than a child's – a woman?" The tracks seemed resolute and direct - apparently with a destination in mind. Sam decided to follow the tracks and see where they led. As he followed the tracks in the sand, Sam kept an eye ahead of him for a glimpse of the one who made them, but saw no one. Suddenly the tracks were lost in freshly washed sand. They were no more and did not seem to reappear beyond the wet sand in any direction. This was much farther than Sam had ever walked before. The beach was not as open as it had been. The wide stretch of open sand was now broken by more and more rocks and vegetation closer to the sea as it rose slightly changing from a gentle slope into the water to a sharp drop and pounding surf. Sam found himself at an outcropping and his eyes began a search of the rocks and up the slope beyond to the base of a high rocky cliff. It looked to be thirty feet high or more, almost vertical, and definitely a challenge to reach the top. The water at the base of the cliff swirled against jagged rocks and pounded against the wall of the cliff itself, throwing surf and spray high into the air with each wave. The trail he had followed ended there. His eyes searched seaward but found no one. Puzzled, Sam looked for a way up the side of the cliff to a vantage point. The sheer rock wall seemed un-climbable, and inland, the brush offered no break that might bring a trail. He was totally stumped, and decided to let it go. He shrugged off the curiosity and desire and to solve the mystery of the vanished tracks. Dismissing it, he turned back toward the cottage and back to thoughts of his problems.

Chapter 6

The next day, Sam decided to return to town. He grabbed his tote bag (just in case) and walked briskly to town. The sandy road crunched beneath his sandals. The sea lapped on one side of him and the wind rustled the leaves of the trees as he walked. The gulls with their ever present cries added a bit of music to nature's symphony of sounds – all lifting Sam's spirits as he walked.

The town greeted him as before with friendly faces and nods. The shops now looked familiar and inviting. Gimmie was on the bench in front of the barber shop, but Sam was pretty sure he was not waiting for a haircut.

Antoinetta stood in the doorway as though waiting for him and greeted him with a "Welcome back!".

He walked easily into her shop and she, again offered tea. Sam smiled and sat to chat with this charming lady.

"How is your stay on the island, Sam?" she asked.

"I am really enjoying the island." He replied, "But there are so many things I have yet to learn…"

She smiled a knowing smile and her pale blue eyes twinkled. "Island life is different." She said, holding her cup poised before her. "…and this is a different island. It will make you a part of itself if you aren't careful." Her words and the accent of a different world made the statement intriguing and mysterious. She sat perfectly straight in her genteel way with every strand of her white hair as though it had been tactically and carefully placed exactly where it was. The hint of rouge and lipstick seemed a part of her flawless face. Sam could not take his eyes from her. She took a sip of her tea and laughed a quiet laugh that put Sam at ease and they began to talk about the weather. She assured Sam that it was always nice – except for an occasional tropical storm that never lasted long. She didn't press for any information about him, but talked on about her own life on the island. They sat through a second cup of tea, as she told him about her late husband and how they had come to the island many years ago. She talked of a time when she felt like a stranger on the island and was homesick for her native France. She had wandered the beaches then, waiting for her husband's ship to return from sea… She paused a long pause as though remembering and then quickly added that the island

and the sea had calmed her loneliness and become her friend. Sam felt a strange closeness to Antoinetta; and when he rose to leave, the handshake was long and warm. She thanked him for stopping by and assured him that tea would be waiting any time he was in town.

Sam passed the other shops, stopping only to admire, again, the art on display. Several new pieces had been added – one of a man walking away on the beach. Although it was just the back and there was no facial expression, it had the definite feeling of sadness or depression. He wondered if that is the way he looked. How could this K person express so much in a painting?

Sam hurried on to Bob Andrews store – more to talk than to shop and he hoped that Bob would be in and not too busy for a visitor. "Good morning, Sam!"

"Good morning, Bob."

"What brings you to town today?"

"Mostly boredom, I guess. I thought maybe you wouldn't mind if I bent your ear a little."

"Let's go to the café, then, Sam, I could use a store-bought cup of coffee."

Bob told his assistant where he was going, and together they crossed to the café'. Sam hoped Mara wouldn't be there – but she was. She met them at the door with her cheerful smile as Bob passed her with a nod.

"Two coffees, Mara." Bob said and headed for a table in the corner.

Mara hurried to fill the order.

As soon as they sat, Bob leaned over expectantly, and asked Sam what the urgency was. "Oh, no urgency, Bob, I just thought maybe you could answer a few questions for me."

"Whew!" Bob said, "I thought maybe you had run into some kind of trouble."

"Trouble? What kind of trouble? Should I be on the lookout for trouble of some kind?"

"No, not really, but sometimes when visitors come to the island, the natives perform a sort of ritual..."

"Ritual?"

"Yes! Have you been visited by them?
　They will lead you off to their village . . .
　　. . . and make you eat strange things . . .
　　　. . . paint you up with weird tattoos . . .
　　　　. . . and do dances around you . . .
　　　　　. . . before making you a present of
　　　　　　one of their young virgins."

Sam looked like he had just been given a death curse and Bob broke into a howling laugh…

Sam realized he had been had and broke into a relieved laugh himself just as Mara appeared with the coffee and a small plate of pastries.

"Cook says those are on the house." She said. "… too late for breakfast and they'll be stale tomorrow."

"Thanks, Mara" the men said almost simultaneously with a chuckle.

Sam was still recovering from Bob's gag as he reached for a Danish and took a sip of the coffee that had been put before him."Thanks, for that, Bob. I had enough to worry about without being part of some ancient island ritual that included young virgin girls."

Chuckling, Bob replied, "I could tell you were ready for something. So tell me what it is that really brought you into town."

I guess it isn't all that important any more, Bob. I have just been trying to accomplish something in my own life and find that I am so distracted by the beauty of the island and all, that I am not accomplishing what I came for."

"Are you hiding from something, Sam?" Bob asked. "I mean, I don't mean to pry, but you seem a decent sort and nobody here is going to judge your past. Most of us have some kind of past that we wouldn't want exposed, I suppose."

"NO, no, nothing like that. I had a lot of emotional problems to sort out, that's all. My mother died. I inherited the farm and suddenly found myself with a lot of responsibilities that I wasn't ready for. There was this lady... she thought I should just take it all in stride and I kinda ran scared, I guess. I thought if I could get completely away from it all, I could sort out a plan and go back ready to take it on. I hadn't ever taken time for a vacation with my mother sick... Now, I find I am more concerned with questions about the island here than I am able to focus on my own problems. I guess I just needed to talk to some-one."

Bob sobered. He could tell that Sam was not in the mood for his humor and he realized that whatever it was that troubled Sam so, was important enough that he had come seeking help. Bob had no answers, but he knew Sam wasn't looking for answers today; he was looking for conversation. He decided to just jump into it.

"Well, there is little on this island to be distraction." he finally said. "It is a pretty boring place. I think you did well in your selection of places to come to get away from it all. Most everybody here other than the natives, is a lot like you – a million miles away from another life - Some by choice and some by happenstance. Me and Penny came here quite by accident. We were so bored with our lives in Cincinnati, that we took a couple weeks off and took a cruise. The cruise was supposed to be a cruise of the South seas. This was not on the list of regular stops, but the captain put in here overnight to avoid a sudden storm. Penny and I got off and came ashore to explore. We wandered too far up the beach and missed the last launch back to the ship and were left behind. We went to the airport to see if we could get a chopper or something to catch the ship, but nothing was available. Neither of us got very excited about it. We got a room in the hotel and wandered the beach for a few days just talking. We discovered that we were more at peace than we had been in a long time. We didn't really have anything back home, and there was a help wanted sign in the store window so we stayed. We didn't know how long we would stay but when the store went up for sale, we knew it was for good. There was a house for sale; my brother took care of our belongings back home and we've never been back. I wouldn't call us an island of misfits, but it is interesting that most of us have stories. Lotsa folk like you come and go – stay for a week or a month or two and go back to their lives. Some of us just stay. Some stories are well known, some are left behind. Nobody pries. Even old Gimmie is accepted and ignored. I am sure he has a story and I suppose when he wants to talk, we will listen; 'til then, he is where he wants to be and that's that."

Sam idly pushed the pastry round and round on his plate with his spoon as he listened. He took small sips of coffee and barely noticed Mara as she refilled their cups. He lifted his eyes when Bob paused and saw a strange look on Bob's face. It was as though Bob had just awakened from a dream and realized where he was. Sam wondered if he had stirred some kind of restless desire in Bob to go back and visit his old life.

"I didn't mean to…" he started, but Bob interrupted.

"No, no, it is ok. As I was saying, nobody pries; so I haven't told anyone of my past or why I am here for a long time. It is no secret – just kinda forgotten. We used to talk about going back for a visit, but probably never will. There's something about this island that makes the rest of the world seem a bit unimportant. We get news and keep up with some of the happenings back there, but it seems so far away that it doesn't touch us much."

Sam nodded. He knew exactly what Bob meant and he had only been here a few days, yet much of what had driven him here now seemed far away.

Mara came back to refill coffee cups, but both declined. She sat the coffee pot on the table and sat down between them. "You guys look like you are solving the problems of the world." She chirped.

They all laughed and Bob reached over and patted her hand. "Maybe we are doing just that." He smiled at her.

She jumped up, grabbed the coffee and as she bounced away, she tossed a quick "Good for you!" over her shoulder.

Sam followed her with his eyes. He knew that Mara would one day have to leave the island to find out for herself what the rest of the world offered, but he knew that Bob had found what he was looking for right here and was content.

"I wonder..." he thought but answered his own question aloud with, "I need to go back... sometime soon."

The two men rose to leave as though they really had settled the problems of the world; and Sam said a hearty thank you to Bob as they walked out into the street. He looked back to see Mara pick up the money they had left and she waved a thank you and good-bye.

In the street, Bob went back to his friendly store manager mode and asked if Sam needed any supplies.

"No, not today", Sam replied. "I Guess I will just mosey back and take a nap", he chuckled. "…suck up as much of this island life as I can."

Bob slapped him on the shoulder and said, "You just do that. It will be good for what ails you."

Sam watched Bob cross to his store and paused to take in the rest of the town before he headed home.

Back at the cottage, Sam sank into the big cushioned couch to rest from his walk to town. It was mid afternoon and the warmth of the day was waiting for an evening breeze. Sam felt a little lonesome. It was the first time he had really admitted it to himself. "Maybe I need the beach", he thought. He never tired of the sound of the waves on the shore. He wandered down close to the water and settled in the sand, watching, hypnotized by the movement and the sounds of the sea.

The sun was low in the sky when Sam stood to return to the cottage. He hadn't noticed that someone else was nearby. In the dusk, he couldn't really make out her features, but by her carriage and build, he figured her to be in her late teens. She sat above him on the dune. She didn't have the look of the native girls – more American, maybe, but he really couldn't tell and when he started to walk toward the cottage, she jumped up and trotted down the beach. He thought it odd, but dismissed it. Later, as he settled into bed, he remembered the girl on the dune and wondered where she had come from and why she had been sitting alone as though watching him.

Chapter 7

The morning sun beckoned Sam to take his regular walk and once again he headed off as usual along the water's edge. As he walked he decided that today he would once again explore the spot where he had seen the footprints. He quickened his pace in an excited anticipation of solving the mystery that he had left behind before. Surely those footprints had gone someplace, but where?

The now familiar shoreline was Sam's friend this morning. It lay naturally under his feet – little features were now a part of his daily life as much as the surroundings of the farm in Iowa had been all his life. He felt comfortable here. He felt as though he had known this place all his life, and yet, like at home, every morning held something new and he enjoyed the discoveries. A dead fish on the beach brought him to pause and question the very subject of death – how had it died? Was it a castaway from some fisherman? Do fish die of old age? Why here and now? What determines when something or someone should die? What happens after death? For this poor fish, why hadn't one of those circling gulls found it? Did the gulls only eat their own kill? Questions upon questions circled in his mind like the gulls overhead – circles with no apparent end. What was life all about?

As Sam continued, he noticed a small pile of conch shells, each with the end broken off – mysterious a week ago, he now knew as evidence of an islander feast. A feast, but this is all the evidence left behind. There is no litter of cans or trash as there would be back in America, he mused.

As Sam neared the spot of his mysterious footprints, he slowed to take in all the surroundings. "Surely there must be a clue." he thought. But nothing looked disturbed or manmade. It was just a bare beach with no evidence that what he had seen before ever existed. There were no footprints. Sam turned inland and climbed the highest dune he could find, then slowly turned around and around surveying the landscape for any clue. Sand and beach grass lay inland. A small rivulet flowed to the sea from somewhere – its source disappearing in the brush some distance away. And the brush increased in size becoming a forest as it spanned toward the volcano far away. Satisfied that he had seen all there was to see, Sam turned again to the beach and the distant cliff. There has to be a way to the top." He said aloud, and he strode toward it.

The sand turned to rocks as he drew nearer to the cliff. The water splashed violently against the rocks and the base of the cliff. From boulder to boulder Sam edged closer until he stood knee deep in water looking up at the solid rock looming above him. His gaze following the wall away from the sea, he saw nothing but thick overgrowth of heavy craggy brush. He could go no farther, so turned again to the direction of the sea and the familiar sandy dunes. His search had ended. Defeated, Sam decided that it would remain a mystery for now and headed back to his cabin.

As morning turned to afternoon, Sam settled again in his hammock surveying the sea. Suddenly the purpose of his stay on the island returned and he decided that it was time to put his attention to that. Sam weighed the options. It had been in and out of his thoughts, plaguing him, ever since he left home, two weeks ago. What would he go home to? What role should he expect when he returned? Should he return to take up where he had left off in farming – as he had tried to do since his father's death? Should he just act as though nothing had happened and resume the life he had always known? What about Stan, the hired hand? – With Stan's help, he could manage the farm and not feel so overburdened. Could he just let Stan run the farm alone? Stan had certainly been there when he needed someone. He had never thought of him as more than a hired hand, but perhaps that was all he needed - Or should he sell the farm and go looking for another life altogether?

And what about Mary? – his childhood friend who had been there through all of the fun times of his life and then his troubles with the illness and death of his mother. He had never thought of her as anything but a friend, but now it seemed he should expect a different relationship. Was he reading too much into that feeling? Would she expect something from him that he was not ready to give? Would she even be there?

On and on the questions rose and fell, over and over, like the never ending waves of the sea. It all overwhelmed him, and still he questioned himself.

"Why did I ever leave and just run away?

What kind of a man am I?

I should have just picked up the reins and seen it through. It would have all worked out; but here I am and I must make some decisions and go back."

Sam had always been a dutiful son, trying to follow in his father's footsteps, and yet he had never had responsibility. Even after his father's death, his mother had taken on the responsibility and Sam had just gone through the motions of things that had to done. He did not realize how dependent he was on them until his mother actually was gone. Even in the Marines he had been a 'good soldier'. He never questioned. He didn't have to think. He just followed orders. Now, he couldn't shake the feeling of being totally alone with no direction. He had never thought of a future. He had just taken life a day at a time with no thought of tomorrow. Could he continue that way now – alone? He began to realize that it was more than sorrow for the death of his parents. It was fear- fear of being alone – fear that he could not make the necessary decisions and be responsible.

Pangatango had been good for Sam. There were no distractions, he could just turn the questions over and over in his head without making any decisions. He didn't have to face any one or any thing. The daily island decisions were his own, but very small decisions. But this could not last forever. It was time to make some serious decisions – make a plan, and face life in the real world. It was the time of reckoning. On his last trip to town, Sam had added paper and pencil to his shopping list. Bob had obliged with a small pad and a mechanical pencil. Now Sam sat at his table and wrote down all of the options he could think of and one by one methodically, crossed them off or circled them as he considered them. He had to 'see' his decision. He had to make it come to life, and not just have it haunt him in his thoughts. But he didn't see it yet. Looking over and over at the list, he still could not bring himself to return to Iowa – not yet. Iowa was five thousand miles away – a different world - and he was not ready to face what was there.

Leaving the list and pencil, Sam sat on the steps of the cottage, staring out at the endless waves as he had learned to do when there was nothing else to do. "Somewhere there lies an answer." He said aloud. "I am like a pirate on a lost island with an answer like a secret treasure waiting to be discovered; and the world is mocking me with the haunting of the waves ever pounding at my feet. I am no closer to a decision than those waves are to reaching the shore. I must just make a decision and live with it, I guess - maybe tomorrow . . ."

Chapter 8

It was late morning and Sam had, as usual, walked the beach mulling his thoughts. He had decided that he had been away long enough and that whatever needed to be solved couldn't be solved here. It was time to make the decision and go home. He would go back and tackle that list. He was on his way back to the cottage when he again saw the girl that he had seen before. It was as though she was always nearby but at an elusive distance. Sam was determined to find out why. He hurried his pace and climbed the dune where he had seen her. She was gone, but her footprints in the sand led over the dunes and away from the shore. Sam had never ventured very far into the island and had no idea what he might find if he did, but today, he was curious enough to follow the footsteps. They led to a path through the brush and into the forest – a forest of tall trees that looked a lot like pines mixed with some wide leafy kind of tree more like oaks. Intermittently tall palms towered over the others. Tangled gray/green brush covered the floor of the forest. The sandy path seemed to be carved out and kept clear by much use.

Finally, Sam came to a wide clearing guarded by palms. The path seemed to end where a house stood alone, shaded by two large leafy trees. It was not the same type of house that the natives had, but more like Sam would call a conventional house - there were no other houses in sight; just the one small house, and a couple of sheds. There was a garden and a well. Chickens could be heard clucking contentedly from somewhere. No one was in sight but Sam knew he had found the beginning of the answer to his questions.

He drew near the house and called out a 'Hello'.

The door opened slightly as a woman cautiously peered out at the visitor. They looked at each other with apprehension.

Finally, Sam broke the silence and introduced himself. "Hello, my name is Sam Malone. I followed the path looking for someone."

"I suppose it was me." She replied. And opened the door wider and stepped out.

"Yes, I suppose it was" Sam started. "I have seen you several times along the beach and most recently just above my house on the dunes. My curiosity got the best of me. I hope you don't mind."

"No, it was me who was curious and I have been watching you. I am sorry."

"No problem."

"My name is Katrina. They call me Kat. I live here with my mother and spend a lot of time on the beach. I used to come to the house where you live. When it was empty I came and sat on the porch sometimes. When you came, I just wanted to see who was living there. I even brought you some fruit when you first came, but was afraid to talk to you at the time so just left it and then watched.

Sam watched Kat as she talked, noticing her beauty – long reddish brown hair and bronze skin. She didn't look like an island girl nor did she have a European look. In fact she was not the girl he had expected her to be. She had looked like a teenager on the beach. Now Sam guessed her to be maybe twenty years old. She was a young woman, maybe 5'5", slim, shapely, and very feminine in the typical island flowered dress that flowed over her bare feet. Her green eyes spoke of some sadness, yet sparkled with mischief.

"I am sorry to be intruding in your world, but I had to find out who you were." He continued. "I didn't mean any harm. It was nice to meet you." He wanted to say more, ask more questions, but turned to go.

"Wait!" She called. "Would you like a drink or something?"

Sam hesitated and then returned. Kat motioned to the bench in front of the house. He sat slowly as though not certain what he should do and Kat hurried into the house and a moment later returned with two glasses of juice. She handed one to Sam and then settled on an overturned wooden keg nearby and sat in silence, smiling.

Sam broke the silence to ask about her mother. "You said you live here with your mother..." He started.

She quickly answered that her mother was away, but didn't elaborate. "I have lived here all my life." She started but but didn't know what to say next.

Sam felt it was his turn and explained, "I have only been here a couple of weeks. I am staying in the Marshal place, as you know – just kinda visiting the island. I really like it here, but don't expect to stay too long. I am from America and will be going back one day soon . . . . So YOU brought the fruit that day? Thank you. I didn't know where it came from."

The stammering short sentences seemed to be embarrassing to both, and a long silence returned as they sat sipping the juice. Sam tried not to stare, but was caught by her beauty and timid smile. He wanted to know more, but didn't know where to start. Finally, he continued the conversation awkwardly.

"So you have lived here all your life and they call you Kat. Is that all there is to it? You were born here, and went to school and everything? Do you work on the island? He realized that he was asking too much and expecting too much information, but his curiosity was burning.

Kat laughed and eased the moment as she quickly replied. "Yes, yes, and yes." Somehow it felt comfortable to talk to this stranger. She realized that she had not really had a conversation with anyone, especially a man, in a long time. She had been so bottled up with her thoughts and fears and bitterness that she had avoided people except for the brief trips to town to sell her wares. "I was born right here in this house and grew up here. I went to school in town and since then I have just been here. I don't really work in town or anything, but my mother made pottery and I painted it and we sold it in town. I guess we never needed much so it has been enough and gave me time to enjoy life. I never thought of much else."

Sam noticed the unfinished pottery pieces beside the bench and on a wooden rack nearby. He remembered seeing the same pottery in town at the store where the wood carver was . . .

– where he had seen the paintings -the paintings!

Suddenly, it clicked!

"Do you paint anything besides the pottery?" He ventured.

Hesitantly, she nodded a slow reply.

"You are the 'K' on the paintings!"

He exclaimed. "I have wondered what that 'K' meant, or who it was, ever since I got here. Your paintings are beautiful!"

"Thank you. I am glad you like them. I even painted you once, you know. . . not your face, just your back but it was you all the same."

"I remember. I didn't know it was me, but it did look like I felt at the time. Did anyone buy me?" Sam laughed.

"No, I don't think so." she laughed in return and added, "I suppose you are still hanging on the frame in town."

There seemed to be a connection that transcended time and age and background as their conversation grew. They chatted on about the paintings and the pottery and it seemed as though they had been long time friends. Slowly the questions and mystery about footprints and paintings and the girl on the dune were answered and he felt like he had known her all the time. Sam wanted to know more about this beautiful woman and her life on the island. Kat wanted to know everything about this stranger that she had been secretly watching since he stepped into her world. Sam saw a young, but mature, sensible, exciting woman. She saw an intriguing strong man who cared about her and her world. Unspoken, they both saw something they had been searching for and wanted more.

Sam remembered the subject of Kat's mother and returned to the question. Kat's smile faded and she sat silent for a moment, the sadness returned to her eyes, as she then shared that her mother was in Australia, ill. Sam didn't press for more information.

"I'm sorry." He offered, but didn't know what else to say. He rose again to leave, handing Kat the empty glass. "Thanks for letting me stay – and for the juice. What was that?"

"Mango, and you are welcome." She replied as she rose and took the glass. "I hope we can talk again."

"I would like that. You can sit on my porch anytime." He smiled.

As Sam followed the path back to the beach and his cottage, his mind raced. What was happening to him? Why had he been so taken by Kat? Where was this leading? He had found the answers to the mysteries and that should be it. He could get back to his problems – the reason he was here. He had to resolve the questions about his life and future. He had a life and responsibilities in Iowa. He wasn't like Bob Andrews who could just leave it all behind. It was time to face his problems and make some decisions. He had been ready. Earlier today, he had been ready. Yesterday, he had told himself that he had walked the beach enough. He was determined to go back and face whatever he had to. . . But now it had all changed. He was suddenly smitten by a beautiful stranger and didn't want to leave without seeing her again.

Chapter 9

Kat watched Sam as he followed the path back toward his cottage; then turned and going into the house, sat slowly on her bed. She felt stirrings inside her and struggled to sort out the feelings. She realized that she had opened a door that she had kept tightly closed for a long time. She was not sure she wanted that door opened again. Thoughts raced through her mind – mixed memories and thoughts of things that had happened long ago and now seemed to bombard her all at once. She remembered how she had been carefree and happy as a child and how that had all changed.

Kat thought back over her life. She had been born to an island woman and an Irish American. Her father had named her Destiny because he said it was fate that had brought them to this island before she was born. Her mother was not an affectionate woman, but she showed her love in many ways and Kat was close to her - close, but not in the same way as with her father. Her father was the world to her. He made her feel like the princess she dreamed of herself. He named her Destiny Katrina, but called her his 'Little

Kitten'. It was his special name for her. No one else called her that. Everyone else just called her Kat. She thought of that happy childhood and her parents. She thought of the day things had changed. She had lived as the happiest girl on the island. Her mother doted on her, teaching her how to be a woman. Her father would come home from work bringing her presents and sing and dance with her. For fourteen years, her father had been her hero. But in the weeks before her fifteenth birthday, things seemed to change. Her father came home less and less. Her mother seemed sadder. Katrina never doubted her father's love for her but she knew something was wrong. As her fifteenth birthday grew near, she became more anxious. It would be the happiest day of her life. It was the magic age for girls on the island. She had heard that island girls went through rituals on their fifteenth birthday with huge parties to celebrate their passing from childhood into womanhood. But the only thing Katrina wanted was to spend the day with her family and to feel surrounded by the love that she used to feel on other birthdays. She wanted to see her father try to steal a kiss from her mother and watch as her mother feigned timidity, knowing that when she did give in, she would enjoy it and beam with happiness. She wanted her father to pick her up high and swing her around as they laughed together. She wanted to feel her father give her a big birthday hug and surprise her with some 'special gift' and say "Happy Birthday to my little Kitten." But on this special day, her most special day, her father had not showed up. Didn't he know it was her birthday? Didn't he know how important it was to her?

Her best friend, Chad had been there and together they had eaten cake that her mother had made. They went through the motions, but there was no joy inside her. She and Chad had been playmates from as early a time as she could remember. He was like part of the family. He lived in town but spent more time with Kat exploring the ocean and the beachs than at home. They were constant companions. They were best buddies. So it was only natural that she would turn to him at a time like this. After eating, they ran to the ocean – their playground.

It was nearly dark when they came out of the water, but a full moon was rising, big, silvery and beautiful. The swim had invigorated her and she was now in a more playful mood. She grabbed her towel and dried Chad's shoulder-length dark hair, then, wrapping the towel around his face, she ran to the rocks at the edge of the sandy beach. When he freed himself of the towel he followed and pinned her to a large rock in mock indignation. His face was so near hers that she could feel his breath on her cheek. For a long moment he remained kneeling in the sand beside the rock, leaning across her body with his head on her shoulder. Slowly he lifted his head and they gazed into each other's eyes. She suddenly knew that she wanted him to kiss her, and at that moment he wanted to kiss her more than anything. He had been wanting to kiss her for a long time. He had watched her struggle through the emotional upheaval that was taking place in her family, and he wanted to hug her and tell her that everything would be okay. But this little slip of a tomboy that he grew up with, was his best buddy and in many ways was still a child. Suddenly, she looked different. In an impulse, he touched her lips with his. She responded with a little giggle and he pulled away. But something was happening. This tomboy friend was now a fifteen-year-old 'woman' and he wanted to kiss her again. As he looked deep into her eyes in the moonlight, he realized that he didn't need to say anything. He lowered his lips to hers and they kissed softly again. For each of them it was a new experience and it stirred feelings they hadn't known before. He lifted his head again and searched her eyes for a clue to what she might be feeling and thinking. Her eyes told him what he wanted to know and he kissed her again, this time a deep emotional kiss that lingered like the fragrance of the sweet flowering vines of the island.

Chad stood and methodically took their beach towels and spread them on the sand between the rocks. They sat close together silently in the moonlight, each in their own thoughts of what was happening. Suddenly for Kat, the world changed. She had become a woman that day. The moon overhead was full and beautiful. The beach was deserted. They were alone. And there was a desperate need inside her to feel loved. Her father, who had been her source of affection was gone. This boy who had been her playmate and friend had just kissed her. In her confusion she wanted to run, but something held her frozen beside Chad. She wanted him to kiss her again. She wanted to be held. Chad seemed to sense her need and turned to kiss her cheek. She turned and they kissed again. For a long time, they lay side by side on the towels in the sand kissing over and over – little pecks and long soft kisses, playfully experimenting with their lips upon one another, then fell back again to lay side by side and silently look into the sky full of moonlight and stars. The night was beautiful, the feeling exciting. In the excitement, she forgot the disappointment of her father's absence at her party. She felt loved and somehow safe. She fell asleep in Chad's arms.

In the almost six years that had passed since, her world had changed. So much had changed. Sitting there on her bed, alone, her mind went back to that night. It was a night that would forever remain in her memory, but not because of the awakening of new feelings of womanhood. It was a night of confusing events that had changed her life forever. She remembered that she had fallen asleep in Chad's arms and then awakened in the morning to find him gone. Her mother found her there, bringing news of her father – news she didn't want to hear. He hadn't come home. Apparently her father would never be coming home again. She followed her mother home and listened as her mother related that her father had left them and the island. She didn't explain the reasons but Kat knew it was a problem that she couldn't solve. Her universe was suddenly shattered. After a wonderful evening with Chad, he had disappeared and now she learned that her father had also left. She had never felt such intense pain. If this was what it felt like to be a woman, she wanted no part of it. She wanted her daddy back. She wanted to be his little Kitten and to feel safe and protected. She wanted to be a little girl again.

Kat remembered how Chad had tried to comfort her in the weeks following, trying to hold her and kiss her, but she had turned away. His attention only reminded her of that night that had been so wonderful and yet ended as it did. He had tried to explain that he left her because he was confused. She wouldn't listen. She wanted no one, and she could not be comforted. She began spending all of her time alone on the beach and on the rocks and in the water, consumed by nature and embrace of her beautiful island. Her worried mother tried in her own way to reach out to her, but Katrina was unreachable. She was determined to never love anyone again. She built an impenetrable wall around herself and would let no one in. Her bitter soul blinded her to everyone and everything. She felt only betrayal and despair. She never noticed the weariness of her mother or how frail she was becoming. She never noticed the sadness in her mother's eyes. Chad had soon grown tired of her rejections and stopped coming around. She went through the motions of helping her mother with household chores and eating meals but spent most of her time withdrawn, alone. She sketched sad pictures in the sand and then with bits of charcoal on scraps of paper – pictures of dark skies and empty beaches, pictures of sad faced children, pictures of sad old people. Her artistic talent was a gift from her father and he had encouraged her in every way. She used to paint the pottery that her mother created to sell to the tourists who came to the island. The pieces were so beautiful that they never stayed on the shelf for long. So now she turned to paintings on canvas as well. It was her one outlet for the turmoil inside her. She took her art with the pottery to the market, and in return, the merchant would provide her supplies of paint and canvas as well as her share of the sales of pottery and artwork.

Kat thought back again, over that year after that birthday that should have been the big moment in her life, but had been so devastating. The year had passed painfully as she went through the motions of life, quietly, solemnly, sadly. She had sometimes spent entire days on the beach with her paints, trying to capture some of the beauty she had known from earlier times; trying to dismiss the loneliness and bitterness inside her. And then, on her sixteenth birthday she had risen before daybreak as usual to comb the beaches and climb the rocks as she and Chad had done together so many times. She had taken her paints, but her heart was not into painting. She was trying to dismiss that it was her birthday, but thinking about the birthday a year earlier, and her sadness was overwhelming; but there was a new emotion stirring inside her. The anger and bitterness had lessened, but more and more she felt the terrible burden of responsibility. She thought of the reasons her father had left. She didn't know why he had left or where he was. Thoughts of blame raced through her mind. Could she have been to blame somehow? She had been so close to her father. She should have known if there was something going on inside him. She should have questioned him. She should have loved him enough to make him want to stay. She wanted so much to tell him she was sorry. If she had been to blame, she wanted to know his forgiveness. She wanted peace.

But a year had passed and that peace had not come. As the thoughts tormented her and tears had blurred her vision, she had settled onto the sand – in the very spot where she had been with Chad on that night, a year before - where she had felt the excitement of a first kiss, and where her mother had found her alone to tell of her father leaving. She remembered how she had been there a long time, just trying to block out the thoughts, when she heard someone speak her name. She had looked up to see Chad! He was different. He was not the playmate of her childhood. He was an older Chad, more handsome than ever. She remembered that she had been startled, and stared at this familiar stranger; waiting for him to speak.

He had smiled a sad smile and sat down beside her, silent at first and then stammered a "I Have been looking for you. I came to tell you good-bye. It has been a long time in coming, Kat, but I have decided to leave the island. I have taken a job on a freighter and am leaving tomorrow. I just didn't want to leave without telling you." With that, he had left – left her alone again.

Six years had passed. Now, after talking to Sam, something had stirred those memories and feelings to surface again. Kat let the memories of those years pass before her. All of the memories and sadness and emptiness she had packed away and accepted suddenly exploded before her again. She thought of all the time that had passed since those two birthdays and how that since then she had become a different person. It had been so long now, since her father had left, and she had rejected Chad and lost him. Her mother was now in some hospital far away and she was alone. She, was overwhelmed by the way they had come flooding back just when she thought she was over them. She thought she was content with her life. . . What was happening? She now faced a new problem – an unexpected relationship that had stirred feelings that she couldn't put in place. She didn't want to renew the expectancy of an experience that she knew would only end with disappointment again. She lay down, and fell asleep with her mind racing; but slept restlessly and woke with the dawn to face another day as she had so many times before – with her paints, on the beach.

Chapter 10

Sam walked slowly back to his cottage. He had solved one of the mysteries of the island. But that was not what he had come here for! He had come to sort out some personal decisions, and now those thoughts had been interrupted with new questions. He had made the decision to leave, but now he had reasons to stay. There was much more about Kat that he wanted o know. He knew he couldn't just leave now. Although determined to live with his decision to leave, he couldn't push Kat from his mind. He went to bed and to sleep, tossing questions back and forth in his head.

Sam woke early and settled at the table with a cup of coffee. He lingered long over a second cup, then a bowl of cereal, trying to decide whether to return to Kat's house or whether to let it go. Finally, returned to what had been his only answer to anything since he had arrived - the beach. He began his usual trek along the water's edge. It was familiar, but somehow not the same. The gulls flew close by crying out mockingly to him. The sea seemed unusually restless, with the waves crashing in foam instead of the usual lapping on the beach. The walk was less satisfying. He walked a long way and turned to come back. He stopped and climbed a nearby dune, as he had many times before and sat in the sand, looking out across the monotonous waves and crashing spray. It had seemed beautiful and majestic before, now it seemed to be just a picture of his mind, with thoughts moving, moving, but going nowhere – one thought rolling into another but never coming to a conclusion.

He thought again of home, wondering what was happening there; picturing in his mind, the farm and the fields, and home. He suddenly wanted to be there again. He had been so relaxed and soothed by the magic of the island in the past few weeks, that he had felt he had almost sorted out all of his questions and was almost ready to return and almost ready to accept his role, but now, there was a new distraction. Feelings that he had not expected pulled at him even as he knew that what he was feeling should not, could not be.

He stared across the water as though looking toward home. He felt homesick. Part of him longed to return to that life, but at the same time, he didn't want to leave this one – not yet. He thought of Kat and wondered at her beauty and charm and the feelings he felt for her. He stumbled over that thought. They had barely met. How could he know what he felt? How could such thoughts even enter into his mind after one short afternoon with her? But she had entranced him and he knew he had to find out more about her. He sat long, sifting sand between his fingers, deep in thought, not even noticing that the sun was already low in the sky when he realized that he was not alone. He saw Kat walking far down the beach, her paint box under her arm. She walked along slowly, head down as though deep in thought. He wondered if she knew he was there, looking down at her; but then without looking up, she turned and climbed toward him. He watched as she seemed to slowly, carefully place each step as she climbed. She was in that long island dress and her feet would disappear beneath it with each step she took, so it almost looked as though she was floating. She settled in the sand next to Sam and joined him in his vigil over the sea. Neither of them spoke.

They sat silently for a long time as though neither knew what to say and neither wanted to break the spell of the moment. They watched the gulls flying high and then dipping low over the water. They were far enough away that their cries were almost as though in a whisper over the breaking of the waves upon the shore.

Suddenly, breaking the silence, Sam said, softly, "Tell me about your island, Kat."

Kat glanced at him and before he could say more, she immediately sprang to her feet.

"Ahhhh, Pangatango...", she began... and stretching her hands outward from her body and twirling around and around, hair fanning out from her face, she repeated it again and again.

"Pangatango...

Pangatango...

Pangatango....

. . . An island of mystery, intrigue, danger, and romance.... It will capture you and not release you... you will become a part of the island..." She emphasized each phrase with dramatic quivers and inflection to her voice like a fairytale story teller . . . . still twirling, her eyes closed, fingers pointing, wiggling, arms lightly flapping, she was like in a trance that had carried her far away, mockingly delighting in entertaining her audience of one. She opened one eye to see if the effect was working, to see Sam, watching, open-mouthed, speechless and totally in her spell...

One more turn and she plopped to the sand as though exhausted and ready to relinquish the secrets of the universe. She turned toward Sam, crossed her legs and reached out and took both of his hands in hers . . . still maintaining her mock role of the storyteller, her twinkling eyes looked deep into his, searchingly, as she gripped his hands. She seemed to be ready to bring him to a solemn vow to keep all that she was about to tell him as a secret for a lifetime...

"Pangatango . . ." she began again . . ."the name means 'Lost Island of the Sea" – Island where secrets are lost and dreams are realized – Island of secret beginnings and mysterious endings . . ."

A faint smile crept across Sam's face, but he dared not let out a sound. He didn't want to break the spell that he was sure was going to reveal much more than he had ever expected. He waited for the story to continue - and continue, it did.

Kat released Sam's hands and started with a low whisper that crescendoed and lowered again into long drawn out dramatic phrases using her hands to emphasize each point as she plunged into the history and the folklore of the island.

"Thousands of years ago, right here in this very spot, the sea gods became very angry. They wrestled at the bottom of the sea and stirred up the center of the earth. A fiery mountain rose up from beneath the sea. It rose high into the sky. As it rose, it erupted, and spewed out a great rain of ash and rocks and sand that created a mountain - a mountain that smoked for a hundred years. The winds blew upon it year after year until the sea gods were tired and went to sleep. Rains came and washed sand and earth down from the sides of the mountain. Slowly storms and rains carried more and more sands from the bottom of the sea and offered them as sacrifices to the mountain. Satisfied with the sacrifices, the mountain laid down and went to sleep. As it laid down, it spread its arms and legs out into the sea to make the island that you see now. It slept for a long, long time, with only birds and sea creatures making it their home. The birds came and carried seeds from far away. The seeds grew and turned the island green. The island lay sleeping with sea creatures guarding it and the birds singing to it. Then one day, a terrible war happened in the islands far to the west. Invaders came and killed almost all of the people of those islands. Only a few escaped in their dugout canoes. They had only the clothes on their backs and a little food. They traveled for weeks, letting the winds and the waves carry them, eating what fish they could catch and drinking rain water from an occasional shower. The sea brought them here where they landed, nearly dead. They found fruit and nourished themselves, then cautiously explored the island until they were sure there were none of their enemies here. When they realized that they were alone and safe, they claimed the island as their new home. They named the island Pangatango – lost island - because no one else was here. Most of the people who live here now are descendants of those lost people. They do not know where they came from or who their ancestors are beyond this island. They only know that their ancestors came here from far-away islands in the west and began a new tribe. If you ask them the name of their tribe they will say 'Pango' – which means Lost

Ones'. They say that the gods told their ancestors that this island was made for them. They say that the island is where they are supposed to stay because it is safe here. Most of them have never left the island. Most of them have never dared to, nor wanted to. They fear the outside world. The ones who do leave, seldom come back. If they come back, it is to tell of an unfriendly world that is not like Pangatango. The Pangos are content to be who they are. They are friendly but will not allow themselves to mix with outsiders. The women do not marry men from outside. The men never court women from outside. They see outsiders as creatures from another world that they do not want to know."

Becoming more serious, Kat went on to talk of a more historical account. "There are stories of Pirates who came here hundreds of years ago, but they didn't stay. The Pangos went to the mountain and hid from the pirates. They feared for their lives but watched as the pirates searched the island. They watched as the pirates gave up and left. They knew that the island was not a good place for the pirates because there was nothing here of value for them and it was too far from the routes of the ships that they wanted to plunder.

The Pangos knew that they were safe. Wars have brought a few other people here, lost or ship-wrecked, but few have stayed. The ones who did stay settled where the town is and left the rest of the island pretty much alone. The ones who came always brought things that they left behind – tools, pieces of things from an outside civilization - even animals,. Slowly those things have become part of our life and our culture. Missionaries came and taught about the God and religion of the other world. Some have accepted that and believed, but it has not changed their way of life. They were a peaceful, happy people before and remain so. The missionaries taught the Pangos to speak English. Others who come, bring their own language. Most speak English. Many of the Pangos still speak an island language. They only speak it in the privacy of their own homes. They will never let you hear them speak it. They do not want outsiders to learn of their customs or language. They call all outsiders 'Visters' – a word they learned from the missionaries long ago who taught them that outsiders were not going to hurt them, they were just visitors and would soon leave. The missionaries left too, but some Pangos still follow the missionary's religion and teach it to others in their world. Now Pangatango is an island of two peoples – Pangos and Visters. No matter how long you live here, if you are not a Pango, you are a Vister. The Pangos will never accept you as a part of their tribe. They will always be suspicious of you. But Pangatango is an island of safety and rest for those who come here. We have a school, shops, a church, and, as you know, even a place for airplanes to bring people like you to us. There are a few tourist ships that stop here for a day. They don't stay long. The tourists have little interest in anything beyond the town. Some stay for a while, but those tourists, rarely leave town. They stay in the hotel. They come to rest and swim or hide from something. They shop in the shops in town, and the natives provide them with the trinkets they are looking for."

Returning to her role of legend teller, almost as if repeating a sorcerer's warning,

"If you stay long enough, the island will become part of you.

If you stay too long, the island will not let you go."

Kat slumped as though drained of all the energy that was in her and sat in silence. She closed her eyes as though in prayer or rest. Sam marveled at her tale and sat beside her in silent reverence. He had only meant to learn about the size of the island, how many people lived there, and what there was to see or do. He knew that she had not really understood his question but let it go, satisfied that he had seen a part of Kat that he hadn't seen before. He also now had many more questions. They could be saved for another time. Sam tried to read in Kat's face whether she had been serious or if she was just trying to amuse him. He decided to take it all in as a true legend and leaned toward her to say thank you when she suddenly broke into laughter. That confused him even more.

She said, "You don't believe a word I said, do you?"

"Of course I do". He replied. "I don't know if you believe all of that story yourself, but since you tell me, I believe. This island is like a fairy land and as mysterious as it is, I believe that your story fits the island completely."

Kat laughed again, A sort of nervous, embarrassed laugh - and then suddenly turned serious. "I don't know what to believe", she started.

"The legend of the beginning of the island is, of course, only legend. I doubt that anyone believes in the sea gods anymore or that the island was the result of such angry sea gods wrestling. The rest, is, as true as it can be. The Pangos don't know of their ancestry outside of this island. And they don't know for sure of where they came from but the stories have been told and retold, passed from one generation to another until it becomes the 'official history'. No one disputes it. There is no history of the volcano or when it may have erupted last, but it is there and it is the belief that it formed the rest of the island by its eruption. The rest is pretty factual as far as I know it. The townspeople each have stories of their own and the Pangos are a culture of their own. They don't mix. I doubt you will ever find out much more about the history of anything. No one seems to really care. The Pangos won't socialize with the Visters but the only story you will ever hear from them is the legend. They don't even tell that to outsiders. They are still afraid of their far-off enemies. When the missionaries were here, they tried to dispel the legend and tell of a creator that had made them and formed this island, but that is one story that they never accepted. After a while the missionaries stopped trying. They only shared their religion of a great God who could be their friend and save them from a fiery hell. When they left, the Pangos seemed almost relieved to have their legend again. The Pangos do speak English and still have their own language as well. Not many outsiders speak their language so if they are to trade or communicate, they need to use the English of the visters. The school is mostly for the townspeople – there is one teacher who teaches a handful of kids. Our church in town is for whoever wants to come, mostly led by regular people who seem to need to pray or worship."

Kat paused and looked off into the distance as if to try to remember more.

Sam quickly responded to the pause and assured her that she had told him what he wanted to know. 'I have lots of questions", he said, "but they can wait. Perhaps we can talk of it again."

Sam rose to leave but Kat remained. She looked at Sam with a quizzical look and finally asked, "Why do you want to know so much?" What will you do with all of this information?" She suddenly seemed suspicious of him as though he was some sort of spy.

Sam settled back in the sand and reached for Kat's hand. "Oh, Kat, I don't mean to intrude in your life or ask questions that you don't want to answer. I am not going to use this information for anything. I am just fascinated by the island and the people on it – especially you. I want to know as much as I can about it. I will tell you my story later, but for now, I am just glad to have met you and would like to spend time with you hearing about everything. I am an outsider and find it all interesting just as you would find America interesting. I hope we can talk often and you can share a lot of things with me."

Chapter 11

It was early morning – the sun just coming up. Sam woke to the sound of the waves on the shore and the cries of the gulls. He lay in bed staring at the ceiling, recounting the events of the previous days, trying to make sense of all that was happening in his life. He had come five thousand miles to spend those weeks walking barefoot sorting his thoughts and just when he thought he had sorted them out, he had new thoughts to sort.

"Why isn't life ever simple for Me?" he mumbled aloud as he rose and pulled his shorts on.

Going to the door, Sam realized that he was not alone. Kat sat on his steps gazing out toward the sea.

Without turning, she offered, "I brought you a basket of fruit, Sam Malone."

Sam quickly dropped to the steps and sat beside her, taking the basket.

"Just what I needed!" he exclaimed. "How thoughtful of you. Can I make you breakfast? How about flapjacks?"

She gave Sam a quizzical look and accepted. He took her by the hand and led her into the house, seating her at the table.

"What are flapjacks? Kat asked.

"Flapjacks are simple but filling – the breakfast of the American plains." He said as he grabbed a box of mix from the cupboard and stirred the batter and turned on the stove. "We should have sausage or bacon, but I guess we will do without it this time. – Coffee?" He heated some water and brought out two mugs and a jar of instant coffee.

"I guess." She said as she stirred her coffee.

Soon the pancakes were sizzling in the frying pan and Sam brought out plates and silver, and syrup. He placed a small golden brown pancake on Kat's plate and noticed a smile that seemed to hide a secret.

"What's the matter?" he asked.

"Nothing, but they look like my Daddy's Irish pancakes."

"Oh, the joke's on me." Sam said with a laugh. Flapjack is just another name for pancakes. "I didn't think you would have heard of them. Sorry."

"No, it is perfect. I haven't had pancakes in a long time. This is good."

"Well, enjoy. And we can have fruit for dessert; a friend brought me some." Sam joked.

Dishes quickly washed, they returned to the porch and the view of the sea.

"I love this view." They said almost simultaneously.

"It is so calming." Sam said, "I have sat here for many hours and just watched the waves, listened to the gulls."

"Me too." Kat responded. "This house is in the perfect spot."

They sat together in silence, then Kat jumped up."Let me show you some of my island." She cried. She ran toward the sea and Sam followed. They started down the beach in the same direction that Sam had walked many times before - chatting about the waves and the gulls and dead fish. Sam picked up a shell and told Kat of his childhood adventures on the beach and his pail of shells that were left behind. Kat pointed out each shell she knew by name as they walked over them along the way. At one point, Kat stopped and pointed inland.

"There is a Pango village just over those dunes." She offered.

Sam replied that he had climbed the dunes once and seen it.

"Did you go there?" she questioned.

"No, I don't think they even saw me." He replied.

"It would have been alright, but they are suspicious of strangers. There are other villages farther inland, most are on the other side of the island."

She quickly returned to talk of the beach and shells. "The shells that you find on the beach are all dead." She said. "Live ones are much prettier. I will show you how to find live ones tonight"

"Tonight?"

"Yes. That is the best time. – but let me show you my special place here, now."

They had reached the place where the shore became rocky and the cliff loomed ahead. Kat ran ahead excitedly. Sam, trying to find good footing in the now rocky shore, followed a distance behind in anticipation. He had been here before and found nothing but a wall of rock. Kat waded on through knee high churning water to the base of the wall and then turned and followed it toward the mangroves - and disappeared. Following a distance behind, Sam stopped in bewilderment. Kat reappeared from behind the brush growing close against the wall of rock.

"Come, let me show you!" She teased.

"I am coming" he puffed as he struggled through the water and over the rocks.

Kat pushed aside the branches, hugging the wall for a short distance, Sam following.

Suddenly they came upon an opening in the rock. It was well hidden behind the branches. It was a narrow hallway into the rock wall. And just inside the hallway, stones and debris had tumbled down over time from the top, forming a steep 'ramp' to the top. Kat quickly showed Sam how she could grab spots along the wall on either side and climb the ramp. Sam followed her, and they clambered onto the flat surface of the top.

"What a view!" Sam exclaimed as he stood and turned from one direction to another.

They were standing on a large flat 'stone' in the middle of 'nowhere'. The surface was nearly smooth, except for chips of stone and some tiny green twigs trying to grow out of cracks in the stone. All sides seemed to drop abruptly into the forest or the sea.

Looking out to sea, it was spectacular – miles and miles to the horizon. Looking back over the shoreline that he and Kat had followed, he could see all the way to town! There was the top of the hotel and the windsock and searchlight tower at the airport! Inland, the island was mostly covered with forest and hills.

Kat beamed. She smiled proudly as she watched Sam 'discover' her special place. She reached for his hand and led him to the edge of the cliff overlooking the ocean. They sat and drank in the wide expanse of water beneath them. The waves crashed below but eerily, because of the distance, they were almost silent as they crashed. Sam marveled at the whole scene.

"How did you ever find this spot?" he asked Kat.

And she began: "I came here when I was just a kid with my friend, Chad. We were exploring and found the crack in the wall. It wasn't as easy a climb then, a lot of stones have fallen since then, making the path up not so steep. It was really steep, but we dared each other and made it to the top. We dared each other to dive into the ocean. I am glad we never did that, but it became our 'adventure spot'. We were on top of the world. No one could find us here. We sat and tried to outdo each other to see who could throw stones the farthest into the water. And each time we came we challenged each other to see who could climb the fastest. I suppose we knocked a lot of chips and stones down ourselves over the years, making it easier to climb."

"How many times did you sit up here and watch me?" He asked.

"You'll never know." She smiled mischievously.

"I feel violated." He laughed.

"I don't come here so much anymore. Maybe I've grown up." She laughed, "But it is a good place to watch the world."

"Come look at the volcano from here." She cried. "It looks much closer from here – like you could almost touch it."

Sam agreed. "Have you ever been to the volcano?" he asked.

"Yes, sort of to the bottom of the mountain; but it is a long hike. Chad and I went once and it took two days."

"Through the forest?"

"There are kind of paths."

"It took two days? Where did you spend the night?"

"We didn't sleep much. We sat backed up against a tree and tried to keep each other awake 'til it was light enough to find our way back."

"Are there any roads or anything?"

"There is one at the other end of town. I don't know who goes there, but there must be some reason because there is one road that goes almost all the way around the island and another one that goes up the side of the volcano."

"I'd like to go. Do you suppose a cab would take us there?"

Kat changed the subject and suggested that they go back down.

Sam, sensing her reluctance to talk about the volcano, quickly threw a stone out over the cliff into the water, saying "beat that!"

Kat responded with another stone – much farther. One after another, they competed, watching the stones fly out and down, down until it disappeared into the water, too far away to hear the sound of the splash.

Sam sat, again cross-legged on the ground with Kat close beside him, and watched the waves below. The sun shone brightly causing sparkles of light on the dancing waves and not far out, a school of porpoises swam playfully by. Entranced by the view and engulfed in the warmth of Kat's presence, Sam felt like a kid on a holiday. He drank in the quiet of the moment. The waves below were so far away that they were almost silent. A slight breeze like a fan on a hot summer day in Iowa nearly put Sam to sleep as he sat close to Kat and waited for her to speak. He could see that she, too, was thinking of some other time and place.

"Maybe we should head back." He offered.

She seemed startled at first, at the sound of his voice, then quickly agreed.

"Do we take the same path back, or is there another way?" he ventured.

"There is another way – through the trees, but it is not easy and a lot farther."

"Then we will go the way we came."

Gingerly, they stepped over the edge onto the ramp of stones and backed slowly down, grabbing handholds as they went. Soon they were back in the water behind the curtain of mangroves, then out toward the open and back to the beach. Kat raced off, splashing in the water to the open beach. Sam followed, stumbling. He grabbed for Kat's hand and she guided him through the stones to clear sand. They stood for a moment, hand in hand in silence, then, releasing, turned and headed home.

Sam turned, looking back to see where he had come from and could not even discern that the opening existed. He marveled that he had previously searched for some answer to the disappearing footprints and found none."Another mystery solved." He said to himself. But solving that mystery was not enough. There were still questions - the questions that had brought him here. Right now those questions could wait. For the moment, he was enjoying Kat's company.

Chapter 12

The sun was fully set and stars were starting to show up when Kat appeared at Sam's door. She had two flashlights and a small bucket. Sam looked at her quizzically as she came into the cabin with her load.

"What are we going to do?" he asked.

"Did you forget? She asked. "We are going shelling."

"I had forgotten." He replied. "So let's go!"

Kat handed him a flashlight and led the way toward the beach; to a protected cove. The water was very calm – barely a wave, and clear as glass.

"This is the best time!" She proclaimed. Handing the bucket and a flashlight to Sam, She immediately waded out into the water, shining her flashlight downward as she went. Sam followed close behind. In knee depth water they bent over searching the sandy bottom of the ocean at their feet. Sam didn't really know what to expect, but Kat seemed to. Slowly they waded, searching until Kat exclaimed, "See! It's a trail!"

The light shown down through the water onto the sandy bottom. Sam spotted the line in the sand that Kat was pointing out.

"Follow it!" she said. It was only a short distance until Sam spotted the small object that was making the line.

"It is a live shellfish, moving along, leaving its track behind it. Pick it up." Kat instructed.

Sam reached down and picked up the small shell, only a couple inches long, and held it under the flashlight beam for a closer look. It was shiny light brown with dark spots covering the rounded surface. Turning it over, Sam could see the shiny white bottom and a moving creature pulling itself back into the narrow opening.

Kat came close and exclaimed that he had found a Tiger Cowre!

"That is a nice start!" she said. "Put it in the bucket."

The next one was long and cigar shaped, with a point on one end and opening along the bottom and other end.

"An Olive." she said.

Sam was getting excited as they wandered along shining their lights into the water looking for trails and shells. There were more cowre's of different sizes and shapes, Cones, all different colors – some spotted black and white, others of striped or multi colored patterns, long auger shaped shells, round humped back shells and one with shiny spines and a wide mouth… On they went, losing track of time and distance, just wading in the knee deep water and scanning the bottom with their flashlights. A light wave would pass over and they would lose the view temporarily and have to stop, stand and wait for the water to be still enough to find their prey again.

Kat looked in the pail and declared that they were having a good night. "Sometimes they are many and different, other times, none at all. We did good." And they are all alive! That means they are not damaged and dull like the ones you find on the beach."

"But if they are alive, what do we do with them?" Sam asked.

"We will clean them and they will be fine."

"How do you clean them?"

"Actually, you let nature do it. I have a box with screens in it that my daddy made for me. We will use that." Put the shells in the box for a few days where ants can find it and they will do the cleaning for you."

Finally, after midnight and a few more finds, Kat wanted to return to the cabin. Sam wanted to continue but reluctantly followed.

"There will be other nights." Kat exclaimed.

But Sam knew that there could be very few more nights, he would have to be content with what he had. He did have some shells that he had picked up along the beach, and he was content. It replaced that forgotten pail of shells from years ago, and it had been a fun adventure with Kat to show him the living creatures in the ocean.

The adventures of the past few days had changed things – Sam wanted to spend a few more days and enjoy the moments before leaving. He had been alone with his thoughts of problems and decisions about home, now he had distractions that pushed those thoughts to another place in his mind. He was not as anxious to face them as he had been.

The next day, Sam was up and anxious for another day. The day before had been exciting, The evening had been exhilarating. He knew it was the companionship of Kat and that it was only temporary, but he wanted more. He decided to spend one more day sharing his life with her before actually making a definite decision to leave.

Sam met Kat on the path to her house. She had apparently felt the need to spend more time together, too and even as he was seeking her, she was coming to him. They left the house and walked the beach again.

They walked together along the beach that had become so familiar to Sam, but seemed different now with someone to talk to. And talk, they did. – Like two friends that had just been reunited after a long absence. All of the feelings that they had bubbled out – from the splashing waves, the sand between their toes, the shells, the dead fish, the gulls . . . they expressed to each other the marvel of creation and how insignificant they felt under the blue sky beside the endless ocean. They settled on the large driftwood that Sam had found on his first day on the beach and talked. . . . expressing thoughts that had been bottled up for weeks. They waded again in the water like two kids and talked. They sat in the sand again and talked. It seemed to Sam that there were not enough words or time to say all he was feeling. Apparently

Kat felt the same. Sam felt some kind of kinship to Kat that he couldn't understand. She seemed to be mature and sophisticated at the same time that she was child-like and exciting. He, too, felt a change in his personality. – the boy in him was overtaking the macho man he envisioned himself to be.

As the two walked, and the chatter continued, Sam realized that there was more to their conversation than just chatter. He was enjoying the company of his companion. They seemed to have found a relationship that bonded them together in more ways than one. She was not just an island girl that he had met and was 'showing him the sights'. Sam's mind raced behind their conversation. He wanted to say it all out loud. He wanted to stop and share his feelings with her! But he didn't know how to say it. It was like he was standing outside of himself, watching and seeing the two of them together.

They had discovered that timeless bridge that somehow welds spirits together in a union of kinship – two lost souls reaching out for the embrace of the world – age and history having no consequence. They both were grasping the moment with child-like abandon. Kat, who had to fend for herself and had become mature and sensible, suddenly found herself to feel young and life to be exciting. Sam felt a change in his own personality – the boy in him was overtaking the macho man he had envisioned himself to be. Shedding his manly reserve, he was eager to find whatever it would be that could satisfy a longing that even he didn't understand. Emotions that he didn't know he had seemed so natural as he shared his reactions to the world around him and listened to Kat.

It was plain that Kat was having the same feelings. Sam was somehow replacing the boyfriend of her youth and the strength of her father's figure. She felt alive again. She felt free to talk and laugh and be open about her feelings and dreams.

There was a bridge that somehow crossed the spans of age and time and background. They became two lost souls reaching out for the embrace of the world. Together.

Was it the island? The island of solitude had become an exciting place of companionship and adventure. Was what Antoinetta had said about the island true?

– *'The Island will make you a part of itself if you aren't careful.'*

He didn't want the day to end. He didn't want the beach to end. He wanted it to go on forever.

The two walked on and almost as by silent agreement, they avoided the obvious subject of their relationship, and the inevitable day that Sam would leave.

As the day wore on and they were returning to Sam's cottage, where the day would end, Kat stopped and turned to Sam. "You said you would tell me about you, Sam. You have asked a lot of questions about me and the island, but I know nothing about you."

Climbing higher up the sandy dune, Sam was silent, but then responded. "I don't think you will be interested, but I will, He said. He sat in the sand and taking Kat's hand motioned for her to sit beside him. He looked out toward the horizon with a faraway look in his eyes. He didn't know how Kat could really be interested in his problems or his past, but she sat expectant.

Then slowly and hesitantly, he began, recounting his life, memory by memory, doubt by doubt and question by question. "One day, I was part of a family, the next, it seemed, I was alone. I grew up in a strong farm family. My father worked the farm day and night. We had cows and chickens, and pigs and big barns and lots to do to keep us all busy. Life was good. We had fun together. My mother was always there. Sometimes she was the lady of the house and sometimes out doing farm chores like a man. My brother, David, is older. He had worked on the farm some when he was home, but he wanted a different life. He went off to college and became a city lawyer. When I was barely old enough to drive a tractor, Dad put me to work and I became his farmhand. I learned a lot from him and can do 'most everything I ever saw him do. – but I'm not him. I'm just not him."

Sam paused and went on.

"As soon as I was old enough, I went off to the marines for a couple years, but never did anything important. It was supposed to make me tough, but I wasn't a warrior. Look at me – too sentimental. When Dad got sick and couldn't work they gave me some kind of hardship discharge from the marines and I came back to the farm and took up right where I left off. Dad was really sick and I had to do most of the work. When he died, I was barely twenty. I really felt his loss, but Mom was there. She wanted me to fill my dad's shoes and take care of the farm work with her. I could do it, but it wasn't the same without Dad. It became a job – work without a real purpose – just going through the motions. But Mom held me to it. She was strong. I guess she expected me to fill the void she felt with Dad gone. I think I failed her. I told her we should sell and get off the farm, but she wouldn't hear of it. Then Mom got sick – cancer. She tried to beat it, but it beat her. A few months ago, she died too."

Sam suddenly stopped talking. He couldn't go on. He stared out toward the ever moving waves; the memories welling up and playing through his mind – the memories of his mother's death – something he couldn't control or stop. He remembered standing over her bed in the hospital and watching the life fade from her. He had cried unstoppable tears that day – tears that kept coming like the eternal waves of the ocean before him now. He had left the hospital with such a feeling of aloneness that he struggled to stay coherent. He wandered around town for a while and then to a church - the church that they attended sometimes. It had been a while since he had been there. As a kid he had gone to Sunday School, and later his mother, always strong in her faith, had tried to take the family whenever she could. Dad was a Christian too, but he believed that he could worship in the fields. Sam had strayed from any kind of concern for religion, but now it seemed the only place for him to find any kind of peace. He had found the door open and entered the empty sanctuary where he tried to pray. The only prayer he could utter was 'Why, God?' Finally the tears stopped but the questions had not.

Kat watched quietly as Sam tried to speak, but could not. It was like he had opened a floodgate inside him somewhere and the memories overcame him. His memories took him to the days that followed that day in the hospital. – those dark days of planning the funeral. – and afterward - how David had come home briefly to take care of the legal stuff and try to convince Sam to sell the farm. Then David, the big lawyer, had left right after the funeral 'for more important business' and he had been left alone with the responsibilities that had been his father's, his mother's - and now all his. He remembered how he had come home from the funeral to a dark and empty house. How he had sat alone in the darkness, head in his hands on the table. How Mary had arrived and sat across from him for a while before encouraging him to come sit with her where she held him and caressed him... he wondered what she wanted from him, what he should do – how to react. It was overwhelming.

Sam stuttered it out to Kat and tried to recompose himself, feeling embarrassed. He then remembered Mary and told Kat all about her – the tom-boy kid from the next farm over, who had been his friend since grade school. - how she had been around in the midst of everything – fun times as a kid and work times later when she would come to help with the hay or harvest. They had run through the corn field playing hide and seek. They had raced their bikes on the dirt road, and climbed to the top of windmill, looking out across the waves of grain pretending they were on the high sea on the mast of a pirate ship. She always seemed to be around and in recent years had been a big help when his dad died and his mother had gotten sick. She had been there through his mother's illness. She had been there every day to help nurse her and help him with chores. After that time in the hospital, she had taken him home, trying to comfort him. He told Kat how even that had caused him to question. – Question who he could, or should, lean on. Even Mary couldn't always be there. He had no one.

Sam tried to tell Kat about the funeral, but again he struggled with the words.

"It was awful." He stammered. "I was supposed to be strong, but had a hard time staying composed enough to even be there. I went through the motions but everything seemed so empty. I hardly heard the words that were said. All I could think about was how unfair it all was. I was expected to just step up and go on like nothing had happened, and I knew I couldn't do that."

"Sure you could, Sam." Kat offered, thinking she should say something.

"You should have seen me after the funeral, Kat. Everybody left – even David. He and his wife drove back to the city. Mary drove me home. I just crashed on the couch like a zombie. Mary stayed for a while, trying to comfort me, I guess, but then left me alone. I don't blame her."

"What about the farm, Sam? Who's taking care of it now?"

Sam brightened and stood. "It's ok, he said. "I hired a guy even before Mom died to come and help me. Stan was out of work and knew the farm so I had him come over to help when I needed it and paid him.

"So you just left it all to this guy, Stan, and left?"

"Yep, I just ran away."

"You ran away? Just like that?"

"Yep, I laid around the house for a couple weeks after the funeral and let Stan do all the work. Then I told him I had to get away for a while and asked him if he could take care of things, he said he could. I told him to sell all the livestock if it was too much for him. - He probably did. I drove into town and had the travel lady find this island and arrange everything, went back and threw some clothes in a bag and left. – Ran away."

Sam looked out across the waves and then turned as if to walk away. Kat jumped up and followed him.

"Are you running away now?"

"What?"

"From me?"

"Oh, no, I am sorry. I just thought maybe I had talked too much and we should change the subject or something. I am sure you don't really want to be with a quitter, anyway."

Kat broke the mood with a quick laugh. "You're crazy, Sam. Do you know that? We all have our backgrounds to run away from. At least you can go back."

"Do you think?"

"Sure."

"Maybe you are right. I guess that is what I came here for – to see if I could go back. – or wanted to, and I knew that one day I would have to go back, but . . . Maybe . . I think maybe you have helped me make that decision."

Kat instinctively gave Sam a hug, and he held her for a long time – looking over her shoulder toward the volcano and the island but seeing Iowa. The volcano and the beach and the peacefulness of the island beckoned him to stay, but something stronger seemed to be beckoning him away.

"There, that was it." Sam thought. He had said it all out loud and he had said that he was going home, but the question was, 'when'?

Kat took Sam's hand quietly, and together they instinctively walked back toward Sam's cottage, then toward Kat's house.

They were silent at first, then as they walked through the little paths between the brush and trees to Kat's house, they began to talk of what the future held. Sam had a round-trip ticket and would go to the airport and make arrangements to leave soon. He wasn't ready yet, but he knew it had o be soon. He had always known that he would one day go back to Iowa and find a life that he could be content with, but he hated to leave Kat. He had learned to love this young island girl. He didn't want to leave her alone. He wanted her to be happy.

"Where do we go from here?" he asked.

She, wisely, replied that they would both go back to their own worlds. She had been fine before, she would be again. He would soon be back to the world that was familiar to him. This would only be a memory. Sam saw the sadness return to Kat's eyes, and he had no words to respond to what he saw.

Chapter 13

Sam woke with a start. It was still dark. Sam blinked and listened. The only sound was the usual sound of the waves on the shore. Cautiously he rose and tiptoed toward the open door, looking out into the dim light of early twilight. Someone was sitting on the bottom step of his porch! It was Kat! He quickly went back and pulled on trousers, then turned on the light and returned to the door.

"Kat! Is something wrong?"

"No, I just couldn't sleep and remembered your wish to see the volcano... I thought maybe we could go today."

"Come in. Let's talk about this."

Kat followed him into the house and they sat at the table.

"Want some coffee or something?" Sam offered. She waved it off.

The volcano hadn't been mentioned since the time on the cliff when he had asked about roads and wondered about going to see it. In all of the fast pace of the following days he had nearly forgotten it. Now it seemed that Kat had remembered and wanted to respond to his request.

"I am just curious. I am intrigued, I guess, because it is there and I have never been close to anything like that. You seemed to not want to talk about it before; what changed your mind?" He asked.

"There are lots of legends about the volcano among the Pangos. Some say there are evil spirits. Others call it sacred and are afraid the gods will not be pleased to have visitors. When Chad and I went, we were just kids and we only got to the bottom and were afraid to go farther. There were no trails or anything. It would be difficult to find your way. I don't know what we might find."

"You said there was a road . . ." Sam ventured. "We could go to town and hire someone to drive us up there."

Kat seemed to still be reluctant, but apparently wanted to please Sam with a chance to explore, so agreed. They decided to walk to town and look for a cab or someone who would make the trip. It was still early, but 'early' was what they needed for this trip. It could be a long day. As the sun was just coming up, they put a couple of water bottles and Sam's camera into a tote and headed for town, chatting about the possibilities of their plan. 'Would someone be willing to take them?' 'How far would it be?' 'Would a road really go up the side of the mountain?' 'How long would it take?' And, of course, 'What what would it be like?' 'Was it really a volcano, or was it just a mountain?

Sam and Kat didn't stop in the sleeping town as they walked through, but went straight to where he had hired the cab on his first day on the island. There were no standing cabs at the entrance to the airport, but they saw one at the hotel – a jeep with a canopy roof and the expected decorations. Sam found the driver, a dark-skinned older man, sitting alone on the porch of the hotel, staring off into space as though waiting for the day. Sam climbed the steps toward him; he gave Sam a questioning look as though he had been interrupted in his thoughts. Sam introduced himself and the driver returned his name as Jorge. Sam broached the subject of a day trip.

"Where do you want to go?" Jorge asked

"We would like to go see the mountain. There is a road to the top?"

"There is such a road, but I have never driven up there."

Jorge hesitated, looked at the skies, and after a little thought, suggested a price. Sam thought it was a lot of money, but agreed and they immediately climbed into the cab and started off - Sam in the front with Jorge and Kat in the back seat. As they drove, Jorge questioned what they wanted to see – what they expected. Sam could only tell him that he was curious and wanted to see what the volcano looked like up close. Jorge repeated that he had never done more than drive the main road, not the one up the side of the volcano, but apparently, he, too, was curious and drove on.

They left town, past the airport, and then around the bay and buildings of the seaport and onto a gravel road. Sam sat poised, upright in his seat expectantly. It was a longer distance that it had appeared and the road was a narrow one lane gravel road through overhanging brush. The volcano loomed larger and larger as they approached until suddenly they were at the very base. It stood like a giant ant hill overgrown with vegetation. There were no foothills, no obvious gradual increase in elevation as they neared. It was just there, rising up into the sky. They came to the road that turned up the side – just as Kat had predicted. Jorge hesitated, then with a nod from Sam, turned and started slowly up the side road. It went along quite level at first and then began to follow the side of the mountain, climbing as it went; a wall on one side and a drop on the other. Jorge hugged the wall side. It didn't look like it was used, but had been carved out for a purpose sometime in the distant past. It was narrow, twisty and sometimes steep and rocky, but passable and the jeep had no trouble making the climb. With brush on both sides, there was little to see, but from time to time, brief breaks in the brush would give a glimpse out and beyond to the world below, stretching out to the horizon. The height, itself, was exhilarating and as they were more and more able to see beyond the road, Sam became more and more excited. Kat sat quietly hanging onto the sides of her seat. Jorge seemed more and more intent only on reaching a destination. – a destination that none of them really knew. The trees changed from tall trees to smaller and smaller trees and then to smaller growth until there was little more than low brown shrubs along the side of the road. The view became clearer and the three travelers could see for miles across the island and sea. Suddenly, the road ended in a level clearing and it appeared they had gone as far as they could by car.

Jorge stopped and stepped down looking around. "What do we do now?" he asked.

Sam and Kat stepped out into the sunshine, looking around them. They spoke of the view – overwhelmed by the sight, but somehow anxious for more. It seemed they had come this far and yet had not 'reached the top'.

"I would like to walk higher." Sam said, pointing toward an apparent ridge a distance away. It looked like the crest.

Jorge seemed curious too, so joined them as they hiked up the rocky distance toward the top. The rocks changed from loose stones to something more like lava than rock and at times looked like they had been melted and then cooled to form the shape that they had become. If it were, indeed a volcano, that would have been exactly what it would have been.

Anxiously, apprehensively, they climbed, and finally found themselves 'on top of the world!' they could see in every direction, the landscape of the island and the stretch of the sea. – and before them lay a deep round valley of trees and brush that looked like it had been there since creation. A mist like a low hanging cloud lay in the valley. Sam stood in awe with Kat beside him gasping at the sight. They had, indeed, climbed to the top of an ancient volcano! Sam grasped Kat's had as they took it all in. They stood in silence. He thought of Kat's description of the island when she had told of the legend of the gods being angry and sending this pile of rocks up from the ocean to form the island thousands of years ago. "It could be possible." He whispered to himself.

After Sam had taken a few pictures, Jorge started back toward the jeep. The sun was high in the sky and Sam didn't want to keep Jorge long. They had found what he had wanted to. It was enough. Although the adventurer in him would have climbed down into the valley, he was satisfied. He stood for a moment and then turned to follow Jorge. He looked at Kat to see a strange look on her face, as though she felt she shouldn't be here. He smiled at her as they started toward the jeep. She didn't return the smile, but cautiously began her descent with him toward the jeep below. The breeze that had been wafting earlier suddenly strengthened to a heavy gust and the mist that had been lying in the valley seemed to rise up and surround them. The sky darkened and immediately, the mist turned to rain – first, a misty sprinkle, then full rain! The trio hurried downward over the wet rocky ground toward the jeep. Kat slipped and stumbled. Sam grabbed her hand and together they stumbled to the jeep and clambered into the back seat together. They were soaked and Kat's hair hung dripping over her shoulders and face. Sam looked at her and started to laugh but was soon sobered when he could see that his two companions were not laughing.

"The gods are angry. We should not be here." Kat exclaimed.

Jorge looked worried. He looked at Kat, as though agreeing. "This is not good." He said. "If this keeps up, the road will get slippery."

But he backed and turned until he was headed back down the road they had come up on. With windshield wipers flapping and the rain blowing upon them through the open sides of the jeep, they proceeded slowly down the road. The gravel beneath their wheels was growing muddy as rain water streamed alongside them downward. Jorge clung to the steering wheel with both hands and stared ahead at the road with a determination. He obviously wanted to hurry, but dared only to crawl along the trail hoping to keep a footing on the muddy road. They bounced over a small rock and the jeep lurched sideways as though to leave the road. Jorge struggled to pull it aright and back into the right direction. Sam heard Kat mumbling something and realized that she was praying. He took her hand and felt the tight squeeze of her fear.

Sam had seen rain on the island before. He was sure it would stop soon, but there was no stop in sight. Relentless, it came down. Leaves and small branches blew across the road in front of them. The wipers were no match for the water on the windshield. Jorge was peering through the rain guided only by the brush and trees on either side to assure that they were in the roadway. The places where it had been a steep climb coming up now were treacherous downward 'ramps' with little for the tires to grip. At the top of the first one of these ramps, Jorge paused to put the jeep in a lower gear and then crawled downward. As the road leveled a little, he paused in silence as though to rest before continuing. They could not see any indication of how far they had come or how close they were to the end of the road and because of their slow movement, the road seemed to go on forever. Sam would have questioned if they were even going in the right direction, but there was no other direction. They were going down and there was no other road. It had to be right.

Sam didn't remember all the twists and turns in the road coming up, but now each one seemed like a challenge for the driver and as he made the turns, the jeep would slide a little on the slippery surface. The wheels would slip and the jeep would slide a little from side to side. Jorge was constantly pulling it from one direction to another. Suddenly a violent twist sent the rear of the jeep off the road and into the brush sideways against the wall of the mountain. It wouldn't move. Jorge got out to see how badly they were situated. Sam followed.

"We can push." He offered.

Kat climbed out to help. Together they pushed while Jorge revved the engine. Tires spun in the mud. Inch by inch, it climbed out of the ditch away from the wall of brush and rock. Jorge urged the jeep back onto the road, not wanting to go over the edge on the other side, and stopped.

"We will go slower." Jorge stated, as Sam and Kat climbed back into the jeep. Sam thought to himself that it would be impossible to go any slower than they had been, but slower he did drive. At barely a crawl, they moved down the road, the rain pounding down on the top of the jeep and blowing in from the sides.

It had been nearly noon when they were on top of the world, now it seemed like hours later, they were fleeing the mountain without looking back, straining to see a break in the weather and muddy roadway ahead.

Kat whispered, "The gods are angry."

Sam brushed the idea aside and replied that it was merely a rain storm.

Jorge said nothing as he battled his own struggle to keep them moving. Sam and Kat said no more. They peered through the rain ahead of them hoping for the nightmare to end.

Finally, the road straightened and they could see the intersection of the main road ahead of them. Everyone seemed to relax as Jorge stopped the jeep. He turned to Sam. "This will require more money." he said without a smile.

Sam knew he was not joking and assured him that he would pay him properly for the trouble he had had.

As they finally pulled out on the main road and turned toward town, the rain stopped as quickly as it had begun. Kat looked at Sam as to confirm that it had all happened because the mountain was angry. Sam said nothing.

"Tell no one of this." Jorge said firmly - as though they had experienced a visit from the devil that could never be spoken of.

An hour later, they reached town and Sam asked Jorge to take them all the way to his cabin. "I will pay you there." he said.

Jorge drove on through town and none of them looked right or left. At the house, Sam hurried to get the money and pay Jorge then he and Kat watched in silence as he turned the jeep around and headed back to town. They were sure he would not be sharing his experience with anyone soon.

Sam walked with Kat back to her house, neither of them knowing what to say. Sam thanked her for making the trip with him. He said it had been a beautiful sight and was sorry that it had ended the way it had. They stood together in the clearing looking at the distant volcano standing high against the sky. It looked different somehow — as though it was looking back at them, but not beckoning as it had seemed to in the past. It seemed to be more threatening and foreboding. Sam wondered at the difference, then shrugged it off and saying a quick good-by headed back to his house.

Chapter 14

Sam sat in his hammock with a cup of coffee, looking out toward the ocean, thinking of the events of the previous day. He looked at his watch and noted that it was Sunday. Another week had passed.

"That was quite a Saturday." he said to himself as he mused over the events of the previous day. It had seemed to have been a very long day, indeed. He and Kat had left early and walked to town to hire a cab to take them on that little day trip up the side of the mountain. He had expected it to be a few hours at most, but it had turned into an eight hour trip. He remembered the excitement of the morning – the expectation as they made the adventurous, uncertain ride up the side of the mountain like the climb up a rollercoaster when he was a kid. He remembered the anticipation as the jeep had struggled on the barely passable road, and the relief when they finally reached the top; and the view from the top, again like being at the top of that roller coaster – only so much higher. It had taken his breath away. He remembered the rush of seeing the island beneath them and the ocean around them on all sides and then the valley in the center of the mountain that had been formed thousands of years before, laying shrouded by a misty cloud – and the absolute silence of the moment as they looked down into that valley taking it all in. He remembered the mist then seeming to rise in the wind and turning to rain - and the look on Kat's face when it happened. He remembered the long, difficult ride down the mountain, and how (he could now admit) that he had felt actual fear as they slipped and slid down the road coming back. He winced as he thought of how much danger he had put Kat and Jorge into. Yes, it would have been his fault if anything had happened. It was his foolish desire to climb that mountain... He remembered how he had been so anxious to find out if it really was a volcano or just some strange mountain; and how Kat had been so reluctant to go, yet did it for him; and how Jorge had to be bribed to go. Surely it would have all been on him. He was glad it was over and that he had satisfied his curiosity, but felt a little guilt about being so selfish in his quest. Trying to dismiss those thoughts, his thoughts turned to the reason he was here on Pangatango, the decisions he had to make, and what would happen next.

Lost in thought, Sam barely noticed the appearance of Kat at his doorstep.

"It is Sunday, Sam Malone!" she announced.

"Yes it is!" he replied with a grin. "What do we do today?"

"I am going to church." She said quite matter-of-factly. "Wanna join me?"

Sam, caught off guard, threw back an uncertain "Maybe." He hadn't thought about church since his mother's funeral. It suddenly brought a flash-back of that day and the things that had turned his world upside down. Now, it seemed a different time and place and the thought was not as dark as it had been. Suddenly confronted with an invitation to go to church he reacted without thinking. If he had had time to think about it, he would have backed away into his troubled world, but the sun was shining, A pretty girl was inviting him to 'go to church with her' like she would have invited him to walk the beach or climb the cliff.

"Sure!" he stammered, "But I don't have any church clothes!"

"You don't need em." she replied. "it is pretty much 'come as you' are here."

"Gimmie a minute." He said, as he climbed out of the hammock and dove into the bedroom to change from shorts to long trousers and a different shirt. He quickly smoothed his hair down as he passed the mirror and slipped on his sandals. "Ready as I ever will be!" He grinned as he joined Kat on the steps and they started off toward town.

"This church – what's it like?" Sam questioned.

"It's just 'church', Sam, don't you have churches in America?"

"Sure we do, but they are not all the same; and I just wondered, since this is a different kind of place from America. . . well, nevermind."

"Its ok. Let me think how to describe it . . . we go in, we sit down on benches, we sing a little, and somebody talks for a while and prays and then we go home. A lot of the people from the town go there. I go sometimes, but not every Sunday. People talk to each other after, but I just leave. I don't talk much."

"Do you have a preacher?"

"Yes, sort of – They call him a missionary, but he lives here and he preaches. Sometimes he is gone and someone else talks. He is nice. He is the one who helped my mother – him and his wife."

"Why did your mother need help? Was she sick?"

"Yeah, she got so sick that I couldn't take care of her. It was before you came here. We don't have a real doctor here – just Mr. Williams. He is kinda like a doctor, but he couldn't do anything for her so he told me to talk to the missionary. They knew somebody in Australia and fixed it up for her to go there. I couldn't go. I got a letter that she is ok. I think she will come back one day."

Sam sensed the sadness in Kat's voice and thought of his own experience with his sick mother. He realized that Kat really was a lonely girl. For all of her independence, she was more alone than she wanted to be. In spite of all that she had shared, he knew there was more to her story. He wished he could do or say something, but decided this was not the time to pry or intrude.

They reached the church quite quickly. It was a small chapel facing a side street in the edge of town – a nice neat, white building with a small steeple and a short walk of crushed corral that crunched beneath their feet as they approached the entrance.

The preacher was in the middle of an opening prayer so they waited at the door for his Amen and then slipped in and sat down in a back bench. Inside, it was as white as the outside – white wooden benches on natural wood floor and a dark gray carpet up the aisle in the middle to the altar. The altar was also white but had gray padded kneelers along the front of it and a railing between the altar and the raised platform. A simple white pulpit with a polished wood stained top stood in the middle of the platform immediately behind the altar rail; behind that, against the wall was a tall rough looking wooden cross. It stood out in contrast to the white walls around it and looked as though it had been made of some kind of old weathered lumber from a shipwreck or something. A small electric organ faced the wall on one side of the platform where a small lady sat with her back to the congregation. The gabled ceiling was simply the underside of the roof, supported by simple wooden rafters, also of stained wood. Four tall, narrow windows lined either side of the room. Sam took it all in in a glance, feeling a sacred stillness as impressive as if in a great cathedral.

The congregation was invited to stand and sing – an old hymn that Sam thought he recognized but he couldn't remember the words. The organist played with a determination and the congregation followed as though they had rehearsed it. The music stirred Sam's emotions as it brought back memories from long ago when he as a small boy standing beside his mother drank in the beauty of a hundred voices in unison worshiping in song. He had loved that, but had strayed from it as he grew older. He was now revisiting those memories thousands of miles and many years away from that church in Iowa. It felt good to be there. He glanced at Kat and saw her, singing softly, absorbed in the service.

It was then that Sam looked around at the others who were gathered. Near the front was Antoinetta, looking more elegant than ever. He looked for Bob and didn't see him, but his wife was seated in the bench behind Antoinetta. Beside her was Flo, and on the other side, near a window was Mara, singing with great voice and animation. He didn't recognize anyone else. There were several families – parents and kids sitting together . . . and the preacher in a white shirt and dark tie, behind the pulpit waving his arms and reigning over all. Another song and then the pastor began a sermon – on John 3:16 "For God so loved the world . . ." He exhorted on 'about how

God loves us all in spite of who we are . . . and how His love brought Jesus to the earth to be an example for us to love one another . . .' then turning toward the cross, he continued that 'it was on an old rugged cross just like this one, that Jesus died to save us all - to be a sacrifice for us so we might have eternal life.' He closed with a reminder that 'no matter what we might have in our life that is troubling us, God is only a prayer away.' Then he invited any who would like to, to come and kneel at the altar and pray. A few went forward as the preacher prayed a benediction.

In the sunshine again, Sam and Kat left the church without talking to anyone and walked the road back toward Sam's house. Kat was the first to speak.

"Was it like your American church?"

"Yeah, not much different at all."

"I liked what the preacher said about no matter what problems we have, God is always near. That is kinda neat. Do you believe that?"

"Sure, I guess I do, but it is hard to understand when you can't see God or nothing. I have heard that all my life, but I never could see what difference it made. It's like things happen that we can't do anything about and God may be near, but He doesn't seem to pay any attention. My mom prayed all the time and she got sick and died. God didn't seem to pay any attention."

"Yeah, I know what you mean."

Suddenly, Sam stopped and, as though he wanted to change the subject, turned toward Kat. "Hey! Do you want to go back to town and go to the café for lunch?" He asked.

Kat looked a little alarmed at the sudden change of mood and the question. "I don't know." she replied. "I have never been to the café." She stammered as if to say she would rather not go back to town.

Sam realized that in all the time they had spent together, they had always been alone. Every meal had been at his house or some snack they had eaten on the beach. It had been pretty simple – sandwiches or fruit, mostly. He had introduced Kat to cereal and milk. She had introduced him to fish right out of the ocean, caught with a small net and cooked over a fire; but just the two of them without a thought of being seen by others as a couple. Now he was suggesting restaurant food. And not just the difference in food, he was suggesting that they go to the café – where people would see them together. Church was one thing – anybody could go to church, but to actually go as a couple to the café may seem different. Except for the trip yesterday and then being together in church, no one had really seen them together. Now as he broached the idea of going to the café, it suddenly occurred to him that this may seem like he was asking her for a date or something. Perhaps Kat's reluctance to go stemmed from that thought. Neither of them had thought much about the fact that they were together all the time, but they hadn't been around other people so there was no reason to think of how their relationship might be perceived.

Kat broke the silence with, "I just don't mix with people, y'know?"

Sam knew that wasn't the reason and tried to think of a way out of it. "No problem, it was just a thought, let's go see what we can find in my cupboard. – And back to the subject - This God thing . . . You said yesterday on the mountain that the gods were angry. Do you believe there are other gods?"

Kat laughed "Oh that. It was just a saying. I didn't mean it. You have to remember where you are… and the legends and all. The Pangos still believe in the 'gods' of the island. They may have been converted and all, but when things happen, they are still pretty superstitious. Maybe I am a little too."

"You seemed pretty serious when you said it."

"Maybe I was. It was scary."

"Yeah, It was a little scary. I am sorry that I talked you into that."

"No – I mean, it is ok. I always wondered about the mountain. Now I know."

"Was that why you wanted to go to church today – because of the scare yesterday?"

"Maybe a little." She laughed.

"How do you know so much about the Pangos? Do you spend time with them?"

"Not much any more, but when I was younger, I used to go to the villages and I played with some of the Pango kids. That's how I know about them. I would sit by their fire and hear the stories.

"Is your mother a Pango?"

Kat looked strangely at Sam and gave a hesitant answer. "Not really. – I mean, I don't really know. I asked her once when I was young and she said 'no', but we never talked about it again. She and Daddy came here from another island, I think. Daddy wouldn't live in town or in a Pango village, so built that house where we lived when they first came here. Mother seldom went to town. She didn't go to the Pango villages. She stayed at home and Daddy took care of us. That's all I know."

Sam wanted to know more. They were at his house by then and Sam asked Kat to come in. She sat on the steps, staring out at the sea. He invited her in to eat something, but she sat silent. He went in and scrounged in the cupboard and found some bread and jam and made them each a sandwich, then returned to sit beside her, with cans of cola.

"Tell me about them."

Kat stared out toward the sea. "Daddy is gone." She suddenly said, almost in tears. "Mother is gone now and I may never see her again. There isn't anything to tell."

"Please tell me more." He pleaded. "Tell me more about your family and your life."

Kat looked at Sam in desperation. "I don't know what to tell or what to believe, or anything."

Suddenly, Sam saw a different Kat. He had seen her as the confident, independent young lady, but he saw her differently now. She was now a sad, helpless little girl. She had been covering her feelings and emotions for so long, she had never really faced the reality of her loneliness and fears. Sam instinctively put his arm around her and she responded by moving closer. Burying her head in his chest, she began to sob uncontrollably. Sam pulled her closer, resting his chin on her head, letting her cry it out.

Sam closed his eyes and let the emotions flow. He had met this stranger in a strange place. She had become a friend, and then like a sister and companion, now, a little girl as he held her, comforting her, he felt like a father to her. He knew that feeling would not last long and he began to be concerned about where it would lead next. Smelling the sweetness of her hair, and the warmth of her body close to his, he didn't know what to do next.

As the sobbing subsided, Sam pulled away and took Kat by the hand and led her into the house, and to the couch. She sat and looked up at him in a way he had not seen before. She seemed to be pleading with her eyes for him to do something – something to make everything right. – something that would heal all of the heartache. Sam again took her hands and pulled her up to him and wrapped his arms around her, holding her tightly. He felt her warm, teary cheek against his. He felt her every breath, rising and falling against his chest. They stood for a long moment, saying nothing as Sam tried to sort his thoughts and control his now hunger for more of this closeness. He struggled with feelings and self control. His feelings were now more than that of a comforting father. Holding her this close, he realized the danger of stronger feelings. It scared him a little. Sam released her and led her to a chair at the table. He sat across from her and tried to regain his fatherly composure.

"I'll make some coffee and we can talk." He quickly said. He put some water on to heat and got the cups and sat down again looking across the table at this beautiful teary-eyed woman. Trying to sound as casual as he could, Sam spoke.

"Tell me more about your father." He opened. "You have never told me much about him. You said he was gone. What happened to him?"

"I don't know." She told of her fifteenth birthday and how she had waited for him to come and how he just never came home. She told of how he had been a wonderful father to her and a good husband to her mother, but was gone sometimes for a few days.

He always came home bringing groceries and things; but that on that day, when she was sure he would be there, he hadn't come and she never saw him again.

"Did you ever hear why?" Sam asked as he poured hot water in cups and stirred in the instant coffee.

"Mom wouldn't talk about it. It was as though she knew something but couldn't tell. I think she wanted to protect me from something. It was strange. She just told me that there had been some kind of accident and that Daddy would never be coming home again. Now, I realize that I never knew where he went to work or anything. Sometimes I want to go to town and ask people, but I am afraid to. I don't know what I might find out. I don't know if he went to sea and was lost or if he just left us." It was a long time ago now . . ."

What was your father's name?"

Kat lightened. "Brian – 'Mr. Brian O'Cassidy' he would say to me sometimes. He would put on his hat and dance around the room for me and say, 'I am Mr. Brian O'Cassidy'; and Mom would laugh and I would dance around behind him . . . then he would swing me around and sing to me. . . We never used the name O'Cassidy, though. He told me that these folk wouldn't understand the O part so our name was just Cassidy."

"And you never knew where he went?"

"No. I guess I never thought about it when I was little and so never asked. I guess I thought he worked on a ship. Some of the other kids fathers worked on ships, so I guessed he did too."

"You said they came from another island. . .?"

"Yes, I don't know where or anything. I just knew that from when I was very little, and would ask, mom would say we weren't Pangos. We were from a different place. In school, we heard about all of the other parts of the world and how there were lots of islands and how people were different in other places and that island people had dark skin. Mom had dark skin, so I knew she came from an island. Daddy was from someplace on the other side of the world where people had white skin and I was special because my skin was neither dark or white."

"So you learned all about the world in school? Did you learn of America?"

"Yes, sort of. I never understood all of that. Mostly, I learned to read and write in English and do math a little. America was on the other side of the world, they said. They had big maps in school, but we didn't really talk about them much. It never made sense to me - how the world could be round and how there were other places. Pangatango was all the world I needed."

"But you said your mother is in Australia – do you know anything about Australia?

"No. I just know it is a big Island a long way from here and they have a hospital there where Mom is getting better. I think she will come home soon. The missionaries sent her to a doctor there."

Sam was becoming more relaxed and wanted to know more of Kat and her family. He could tell that she was more comfortable with the subject too. He made them each another cup of coffee and brought out a box of cookies from the cupboard. He told of how he had lived on a big farm that grew lots of crops and animals and how he had traveled here to think when his mother died. Kat listened, in wonder to the description of his life in America. She had known nothing of the outside world and it seemed a fantasy to her.

Sam ventured again. "So tell me more of your school."

"I think I told you everything. When I was little, Daddy taught me to read and write and how to draw, so when I started to school, I already knew most of that stuff. At school we just did the same stuff except we played games and sang songs. We were supposed to go every morning until noon, but I didn't go all of the time. Sometimes Chad and I would go exploring instead." At the mention of Chad, Kat grew wistful and trailed off.

"Who was Chad?" Sam asked.

"I told you about him." He was my best friend. We used to explore all the time – like up on the cliff, and hiking to the mountain."

"Oh, Yeah, but where is he now?"

"He moved away." Kat said matter-of-factly.

It was late afternoon and Sam broached the subject again of a meal. "Let's find something to eat." He suggested. "I will go to town and get some stuff and you can wait here. I won't be long."

Kat smiled. "Let's go fishing!" she replied. "I will go get my net and come back. We'll build a fire on the beach."

They looked at each other as if trying to decide which option to choose.

"Let's do both!" Sam suggested. "I will go to town and get some things while you go for your net, and we will meet back here in a while and cook a nice Sunday Dinner."

Sam watched as Kat headed over the dune toward her house. She seemed a different person than he had first met. Her long dress followed the shape of her body, her hair seemed more radiant than before as she tossed her head a little with each determined step. He wanted to follow and take her hand. He remembered the warmth of her body that he had felt earlier. He wanted to be closer to her.

Sam's mind raced as he jogged along the road toward town. It had been so nice to be close and feel Kat in his arms. 'Was he falling in love with this island girl? Had he lost all senses? What about home and the farm? What about Mary? He had to leave Pangatango. He had to come back to earth and face the real world. This was all just a fantasy that was getting out of hand. . . as he approached the town's shaded streets and welcoming surroundings, he slowed to a walk and tried to put the thoughts aside. Antoinetta was not on the steps. The touristy shops were not open. The barber shop was closed. There was no activity in the street. He had not been in town on a Sunday before. He realized that it was later in the afternoon than he had realized. His mission had been for nothing. He would go back empty handed. It looked as though everyone was taking the day off. As he neared the grocery store, he could see that it, too, was closed. But the General store was open. Flo was sweeping the steps and greeted him as he approached.

"What brings you to town on a Sunday afternoon?" she asked.

"I was just walking". . . he lied, "...and thought maybe – if you are open – I might find a couple of cans of something for this evening."

"Of course" she replied. "Come in and find what you need." She left her broom leaning against the door jamb and led him inside. He quickly searched the grocery shelves and selected some cans of vegetables, Green beans, broccoli. . . and a couple cans of cola. Then he noticed a box of rice... "Perfect" he thought and made his purchase. Stuffing in into a bag, he thanked Flo and headed home.

Kat was waiting for him when he arrived and looked at the things he had brought. She had already filled a tote with pans and plates and everything they could possibly need to have a beach cook-out. She handed Sam the tote and a jug of water, then picked up her own tote of fishing gear and led him toward the beach. She headed in the opposite direction from the path Sam usually took and into an area where he had never been. Between the road and the water a short distance from his house lay a stand of trees and brush that separated the road from the water. Kat led Sam along a little trail through the brush to a small cove hidden from the road, bound by sand bars on two sides and open to the sea. A trickle of water flowed from the island into the cove.

"This is perfect for fishing", she explained. As she settled the bags on the sand "It is deep in the middle and shallow around the sides. Fish like to feed here. No one ever comes to bother them so they feel safe. I came here with Chad a few times."

Sam noticed a small pile of rocks and evidence of a previous campfire near where Kat had stopped. Kat instructed him to start a fire between the rocks. Sam hurriedly found some dry sticks and did as he was told. Kat rearranged the rocks to form support for the two pans she had brought as Sam looked around for more wood. Soon they had a blazing fire. Kat took out her small net and readied for the catch. She had shown Sam before how to throw the round net out over the water and pull the cord and bring it back full of fish. He had watched in amazement as the net settled like a circle on top of the water and then slowly settle out of sight and how she had known just when to pull and close the net around the unsuspecting fish. Sometimes it had been empty or with nothing worth keeping; other times, nearly bursting with the struggling, writhing silver creatures. He settled onto the sand to watch the spectacle again. He had seen her so patiently perform this simple island ritual, but he watched now as though for the first time.

Kat waded out a short distance in the shallow water and deftly cast the net over the deeper water beyond. She paused for only a few moments as the net settled and then with a steady pull on the cord, braced for the weight of the catch. It came back almost empty! She opened it and let the catch go, apparently not satisfied. Sam laughed. Undaunted, she moved farther out toward the sea and cast again and stood motionless, waiting, then suddenly pulled - and braced. This time, it was different. Sam could tell that the weight was greater and he ran out to help her pull it in. Bringing the full net to shore, they spread it out on the sand and selected two nice sized fish 'just right for frying' and let the others go back into the water. Sam watched as they hurried to their freedom.

While Kat quickly cleaned the fish and put them in the frying pan, Sam put the rice and vegetables on to heat. It wasn't long until they were enjoying a feast fit for a Sunday dinner. Both seemed very satisfied and content. Silently, they lingered over the meal and watched the dying embers of the fire and the gulls circling overhead as though waiting for leftovers.

As the sun began to set, they gathered their things and made their way back to Sam's house and settled briefly on the porch before Kat thanked Sam for a nice day, and left for her own house. Sam washed and put the dishes away and sat at the table with a cup of coffee rehearsing the events of the past week.

Sam had watched Kat go over the dunes toward home. She seemed more troubled than usual and he was concerned. He was troubled by Kat's story of her parents' absence. She had mentioned, again, how she wondered what had happened to her father and wondered how her mother was doing. How could a teenage girl be left alone to shift for herself? It was a story too close to home for him. He knew what had happened to his father and mother and here he was on a remote island trying to sort out his feelings about their deaths, while a young girl, alone with no family or friends to turn to, had to deal with the absence of her mother and the mystery of a missing father. Accepting the fact that her mother was a thousand miles away in a hospital or something would be frustrating, but the fact that her father had just disappeared with no rhyme or reason was the most troubling. She needed some closure, he thought, and perhaps he could help bring that to her.

Sam moved to the hammock and sat down. "Before I leave this island, I have to at least try." He said aloud. "but where do I start?"

As he stared out at the sea and the setting sun, Sam realized that he would have to formulate a plan. He couldn't let Kat know what he was doing. He didn't want to get her hopes up or open an issue that would be more than she needed. He had to find a place to start.

"Maybe Bob! If anyone would know where to start, it would be Bob. Tomorrow I will go to town and have a chat with Bob." He decided.

Chapter 15

The sun was barely up as Sam headed for town. He walked a little more briskly than usual. He had a mission and was anxious to get started. The shops were just opening as he reached the edge of town. Antoinetta was nowhere in sight. Only a few residents were visible beginning their day. Sam knew he was early and Bob's store would probably not be open yet, but he was ready to be there when it did open. He stopped at the art shop which had already put Kat's paintings on display. There were a few new ones! He wondered when Kat had had time to do them. It seemed like they were together all the time and he hadn't seen her with her paint box. But he noticed a picture of a familiar piece of driftwood that he had sat on when he first came to the island. And a small painting of a dead fish lying in the sand. She had captured the sadness of the sight and made it a work of art.

As Sam turned again to the street, he saw Bob on the doorstep of his shop, greeting the morning. As he turned to go back into the store, Sam hurried toward him. Bob noticed and stepped down to meet him.

"What brings you to town so early?" he asked.

"I have a problem." Sam replied.

"A grocery problem or a café and coffee problem?"

"I think it may be a problem in private."

"Ooooh, sounds serious. Ok, let's go to my office. Come on inside."

Bob led the way past the shelves of groceries and through a door in the back of the store. It led to a hallway and the back door of the building. There were doors on either side of the hallway, Bob entered the one on the right, exposing his office. It was a small room simply furnished with an old desk and chair and an old worn leather couch at one side; and a pair of file cabinets and a straight chair on the other. The room was exceptionally neat. Except for a few papers on the desk, it looked as though no one ever used the room. The desk faced a window on the opposite wall through which was a view of the sea. Sam had not realized before how close the shops were to the sea. He just hadn't thought about it, but realized now that like the hotel, they were not far from the ocean and if situated right could command a nice view. Bob motioned Sam to the couch and he sat down behind the desk.

"I don't spend a lot of time here.", he explained. "I don't do much business here – most of it out in the store where I can keep an eye on things. But sometimes, I come here to be alone to look out at the sea, - or to take a nap he said with a wink, looking toward the couch."

"So, you said a private problem. Is it money?" he asked.

"No, no, nothing like that. I am just trying to solve a mystery"

"Hmmm, not sure I can help you with mysteries, but sounds intriguing. Tell me more." He said with a grin.

"Well, I know you have told me that people here don't ask questions, and I appreciate that, but I am hoping you can answer some questions that I have."

"Shoot, Sam. I'll give it a try."

"Let me start at the beginning… I met a girl on the island. . ."

"I know." Bob interrupted with a smile. "I told you we don't ask questions or pry, but I didn't say we don't observe."

Caught off guard with that, Sam stuttered and then started, "No, no, it is nothing like that, Bob. I guess I don't have to tell you who the girl is, but there is nothing going on. We have just become friends and she has told me a lot about the island. – and about herself. We seem to have some things in common. We both seem to be without parents and have been questioning some things."

"You have my curiosity, Sam. What is your mystery?"

"Well, Bob, since you seem to know all that goes on, maybe it isn't a mystery to you, but it is to me." Sam began to unfold the events of his conversations with Kat. He told of the stories that Kat had shared about her mother and how she had become sick and had been taken to Australia for treatment – and about her father and how he had mysteriously disappeared. "I don't know how Kat could have just been left behind with no one to turn to. It appears that it was partly her choice and partly some kind of mix-up that she doesn't know how to unravel. She believes that her mother will get well, and come back. I suspect that she is unconsciously hanging on to a hope that her father will one day come back too."

Bob grew serious. He looked out the window toward the sea as though trying to gather his thoughts and formulate an answer. After a long silence, he began."Sam, you are an outsider. I told you we don't pry. We live and let live here. You are seeing things as an outsider. That's not bad, but it is a difficult thing to answer. You are partly right. I do SEEM to know all that goes on. Truth is, I DON'T. I do know most everyone in the area. Sooner or later, they come in and buy stuff and I know names and who's who in what family, but that is about as far as it goes. I don't have all the answers to your mystery, but I do have some ideas of how to find some answers. Let me begin with your Kat. She is a beautiful young lady and I am sure you have been caught up by her. I believe you when you say there is nothing going on, but you may be too close to her to react as we do here on Pangatango. We are not unfeeling, but we don't get involved in other folks' lives. What Kat told you sounds pretty close to right, but fact is, I don't know much more than she does – maybe less.

Kat was about fifteen when her father left but more than eighteen when her mother left. There is little known about her father, but her mother did go to a hospital in Australia. When she went, it was thought that she would be back soon and Kat insisted to stay and take care of the house while she was gone. Kat has proven that she can certainly take care of herself and provide for herself. Have you seen her paintings? I am sure she is earning enough to support herself. She chooses to live alone out there and no one is going to force her to anything else. She had a boyfriend for a while, but he left and she has not been seen with anyone else since. She is a little like Gimmie. She keeps to herself and seems content with that. You are a rare one to get that close to her."

Bob paused then went on, "So, now about her father; and your real mystery. It is a mystery to all of us. I told you, a lot of people have reasons for being here. We don't ask much. Brian was a nice fellow. He came here often for groceries, maybe once a week, usually on Friday. He was always friendly and talkative but never about himself. He talked about what a wonderful day it was and that he was glad to be alive. He would come in with a cheerful greeting and shop around like he needed something special, but usually just took staples. He usually would look for some little bit of candy 'for his little kitten'.

He paid with cash and left with a grin, and a tote sack over his shoulder. I don't know where he came from originally. He had a bit of an Irish sound in his voice, but the story was that he and his wife came here from one of the Indonesian islands. They came just after we bought the store here, so that has been some twenty years. Kat was born soon after, I think. Brian built the house out there, himself. I never saw it. He had some lumber shipped in, I know - hauled it out there with a horse or something, a little at a time because there isn't really any road. He hauled it in through the woods. He put down a well, I guess, but no bathroom or nothing. They live pretty primitively. A lot of folks do. That is why most people live in town. You are an exception. Water and electric goes out to your place and that is the end of the line. Anyone else who lives out of town don't have those things. Don't tell anyone, but I think your sewer is just piped out to sea. Like I said, we don't ask."

"Where did Brian work?"

"Don't really know. I 'spect it was something out of the harbor there – as a hand at the harbor or on a ship. There aren't a lot of jobs, I don't think; but it seems that the harbor does support quite a few folk."

"So . . . the big question – what happened to him?"

Bob didn't answer.

There was a long silence and Sam asked again."What happened to him, Bob?"

Bob seemed a little embarrassed at the question. "Sam, I don't know. Sometimes not asking questions seems right, and sometimes it isn't so right after all. I don't know what happened to Brian Cassidy. Plain and simple, I just never asked and no one said anything. One day he just stopped coming in and that was that. If there had been some gossip or big story, I would have heard, but folks don't gossip much and there was no big story. He was here most every week for years and then not so often and then not at all."

"So you weren't even curious?"

"I suppose so, but lots of people come and go. Life goes on. Knowing can't change anything. There is a word here – 'whahilia' - don't know where it came from, probably the Pangos, but it roughly means: 'what is, is'."

Sam didn't know what else to ask, but expressed his frustration aloud. "A man just leaves his family and disappears and no one even asks."

"It isn't that, Sam. And maybe it is just me. Maybe I just don't ask, - y'know? It wasn't any of my affair and the less I knew, the better. I keep out of trouble by not stickin' my nose into other people's business. Maybe the whole town knows stuff that I don't. But it is a very quiet existence here. We live with Whahilia."

"I don't understand that."

"OK, Sam, The only way I know you are here is because you are here right now. But you are here today. Suppose you don't come into the store tomorrow, and I don't see you again. . . It may be a day or a week or a month, and you just don't come in. I will never know if you went back to Iowa, or to some other country, or fell off that cliff down the beach there. I could ask around, but if no one saw it happen, I wouldn't know. And even if someone did know you got on a plane, I still wouldn't know much. And if they said you told them you were heading for Iowa, I wouldn't know if you made it, and knowing or not knowing wouldn't change my life a bit. I would still be here selling beans and rice to whoever came in that door. Back in Cincinnati, we thought it mattered. We had to read the news every day. It seemed important. Here it doesn't. What is, is. What we know, we deal with, what we don't know seems a bit like a waste of time to think about. If someone dies, we bury them and mourn with the family for a while over the loss, but if someone disappears, we figure they just went away and that is that. Lots of people are here for a while and then gone. It doesn't change anything."

"Ok, I get that, but don't you just want to know about Brian? – just curiosity?"

"I suppose, but suppose Brian had another woman, or suppose him and the missus just had a fight and she told him to leave, or suppose he fell off a ship and drowned or suppose he was picked up by the law on some other island and is in a jail someplace. There is not much consolation in me knowing that. I couldn't change it. Best thing I can do is move on to the next day and not worry about it."

"Don't you think Kat should know?"

"Maybe you're right. Maybe she should know, but it wouldn't change much. She would just move on with her life, and she is doing that now."

"But she would know where to go and what to do if she was sure her father could be found."

"Or if she found out that he run off on purpose, she would be crushed for the rest of her life. . ."

"I understand that possibility, I guess, but . . ."

"Sorry, Sam, I just don't have your answers."

"I haven't talked to many people here, Bob, is everyone like that? Does everyone live with this Whahilia or whatever?"

"Maybe. I don't know. Pretty much, I think. Some stuff we just seem to know – like you being here in the Marshall place... but nobody asked why. Nobody whispered about you. You shared a bit with me, but I didn't share that with anyone else. Truth is, people don't talk much at all here, 'cept about what they need to – if they need something or just to pass the time. I think that is why we are here. We like that atmosphere."

"That sounds great, Bob, but people are people. Surely there is some gossip. What about at the barber shop? – or the bar? What about church? What about when babies are born or somebody dies?"

"Yeah, I guess you are right. I've seen people coo over a new baby and all gather round when somebody dies, but not to the point of pryin' into how it happened. Did anyone seem concerned about what you were doing out there in your little cottage? Nope. You were there and it was your business. I think it carries over somehow from the Pangos. They have their lives and don't want to be disturbed. We have ours.

You ask about the bar – hmmm that does seem strange, I guess; sometimes there is a lot of noisy talk in the bar, but it never seems to spill out. The bartender is a quiet guy. I suspect he listens a lot, but don't talk much."

"So, I am sorry to be bothering you about my questions, Bob. It is just that you are the only one I have really talked to and it seemed natural to start with you."

"Yeah, and I did say that I could tell you someone who might be able to have some answers for you. . . sorry it isn't me, but maybe someone else can help. There is a guy out at the harbor who has been there forever and I am sure knows everyone who has ever come or gone out there. Go talk to Barry Duffield."

With that, the conversation seemed to be over and Bob stood up, apparently anxious to go to work.

Sam interrupted the departure with another question.

"Sam, a few years ago, a military plane landed here in trouble. They had to stay a few days – lived in the hotel. . . Did you know about that?"

Bob rubbed his head for a moment and then, "Yeah, I remember. It was probably five or more years or so. I never met the guys, but did hear that it happened. Why?"

"Oh, no reason. I knew those guys. They told me about this island after it happened and that is how I come to choose to come here. I just wondered if you knew about it."

Bob forced a little smile. "I see, you were testing me to see if I really don't know what goes on around here. Well, there is your answer. I knew and I didn't. I know it happened but there was little talk about it. They were here for a few days and then gone. That was that. - Like everything else here. Whahilia."

"I hope you can find your answers, Sam. Let's go face the day."

Sam stood and paused to take another look out the window. "What a life", he thought to himself.

He repeated "Barry Duffield?" as they walked through the store and Bob nodded.

"I am sure you will find him down at the harbor."

Sam stood in front of the store contemplating what he had just heard and his next move, then turned toward the harbor. It was a long walk but Sam had nothing else to do, and he did want to solve Kat's mystery.

Chapter 16

As Sam approached the harbor, he could see that there was a lot more going on on this little island than he had previously realized. He had been on the road and gone around the harbor when he and Kat had made their trip to the volcano, but he didn't take it all in at that time. They had passed it early in the morning with his goal on his mind and then returning, wet and tired, he certainly had little thought of the activities of the harbor as they passed. Now, walking, Sam had more time to consider the sights. It was a natural bay from the ocean, perhaps a quarter mile wide at the mouth with a long channel extending into the island. The whole channel and bay looked to be nearly a mile. The road met the bay just where it widened, and turned to parallel the narrower channel. Looking out toward the ocean, Sam could see the bay's entrance with structures that looked like small lighthouses on either side where it met the sea. Some of the shore along the bay was open, and some was overgrown with the typical low shrubbery and trees. He passed a driveway that led to some wooden piers for small private boats; then some buildings glimpsed through the brush and an apparent pier for larger sea-going vessels. Sam suspected the channel must be quite deep to allow ships of any size to enter. He walked along the road looking for any break in the undergrowth, or the entrance to some official business or something. There were small warehouse type structures with their backs to him but no buildings that faced the road. Finally Sam found a driveway leading to what appeared to be the area he wanted. Past the brush and buildings, lay an open area piled high with pallets and containers and a busy loading area. A small freighter was tied alongside a long wharf and several people were busy carrying boxes from the ship. A small man with a clipboard was watching the operation. Sam approached him.

"I'm looking for Barry Duffield." Sam announced.

The man turned and looked him up and down and said, "You've found him. What do you need?"

"Just a few minutes of your time." Sam replied. Not wanting to rush into anything, Sam added, "looks like a busy place." and nodded toward the activity around him.

Barry lowered the clipboard and moved closer. "Yeah, some days more than others. It comes and goes." He motioned toward all the containers and boxes. "Today is one of the busy ones. Sometimes we might go for a month with nothing to do."

"Well, then, perhaps there would be a better time, but have you time for just a couple questions?"

"If you can wait a half hour or so, I will be glad to talk to you." He said without taking his eyes off the packages coming off the ship and onto the piles.

Sam agreed and walked off a distance to observe the operation and look more closely at the harbor in general. Sam had never been around any kind of naval shipping / loading operations so it all fascinated him. The closest he had been to anything like that was when they hauled grain to town back in Iowa. This was definitely different.

The small ship that was being unloaded was the only one in the harbor. He assumed that this one would soon be going back to sea. The ship's officers stood ready on the bridge and the crew stood at the rail as though anxious to move on. Light smoke rose idly from the single smoke stack in the middle of the ship. Those not assisting in the unloading, were busy coiling ropes and latching down hatches. When the last package was ashore, Barry met with one of the ship's crew, signed some paperwork and the crewman climbed the gangway that was then quickly hoisted up and clear of the wharf. The crewman with the papers, signaled to the captain on the bridge who, in turn, gave quick orders to crewmembers standing by the lines that held the ship to the pier. Barry's men untied the ship's mooring lines and they were quickly pulled aboard the ship. The men all waved to each other, the smoke from the smokestack suddenly turned black, and grew heavier, a bell sounded from somewhere, a whistle blew, the water churned beneath the stern of the ship and it edged away from the wharf. With the captain on the bridge, giving orders, the ship slowly crawled along the wharf and into the center of the channel and backed slowly out toward the ocean. Sam watched as it reached the end of the harbor, and turned around. The smoke stack blew a new column of black smoke, the whistle blew a long blast, and the ship headed toward the horizon.

Barry, spoke briefly to his men and turned to Sam. He was a small man, maybe a hundred-fifty pounds, dressed in a khaki shirt and denim jeans. He had a serious look on his face partly covered by a shock of brown hair covering his forehead and ears. Without a smile he extended his hand.

Sam introduced himself and began slowly. "I don't really know where to start. I am trying to find out some information about Brian Cassidy."

Barry looked at him curiously and led him to an overturned wooden crate by the warehouse, motioned to Sam to sit and he sat next to him, still watching his men move their boxes into the building with a hand truck. He didn't speak at first, then cautiously eying Sam, asked why he wanted to know.

Sam quickly tried to reassure him that he was not an investigator or anything, just trying to find Brian for his daughter. "I didn't say before, but I am just here for a vacation", Sam shared. "I heard of this island and came to escape from my busy world for a couple weeks. It has turned into longer, but I plan to leave soon. I met Kat on the beach one day and she told me of her father. I am maybe too curious, but had to try to find some information."

"Kat?"

"Yeah, she doesn't know I am here or anything, but she has been long curious about the disappearance of her father and I am wondering if you might know something that would put her mind at ease."

"You are new here, Sam. Maybe just passing through, but not many folk around here ask questions if it don't concern them. So, why are you so interested?"

Sam hesitated, and then started: "Yep, I am new – and just passing through, and I know it ain't my business, but Kat shared her frustration of not knowing about her father. I recently lost both my parents and I can relate, sort of; so I thought I would see if I could find some answers for her. She don't know I am here and I won't tell her anything unless it could do her some good." Going on, "She said she never knew where her father worked – was it here?"

"Sam, I am sorry, I really don't know much that can help you – or her - find him. He worked here some, way back when, (nice guy). He spent a lot of time just hanging around, helping out wherever he could. He was here a long time - Then he signed on with a tramp steamer like the one you saw here today. They were pretty regular, in and out and he was home pretty often, then the ship stopped coming and so did he."

"So what do you know of the ship?"

"Not much. Some of those guys carry questionable cargo and have to keep on the move a lot."

"Do you know the name of the ship?"

"Sure, it was the 'Seadragon'. All one word – I don't know where it home-ported. Some of those ships keep moving, never return to their home port. They pick up cargo from other ships too big or busy to come to the small ports. If there is questionable cargo, they have to keep out of the major ports. I don't know about the Seadragon."

Sam was disappointed. He had gained some information, but it didn't find Kat's father. "Well, thanks, Barry." Sam finally said. "I guess that is all I came for." – but he wanted to extend the conversation. He paused for a moment, then, "Tell me about this place Barry, – How long you been here?"

Barry suddenly relaxed a little and leaned back against the building and stared off into the distance. "I've lived on the island most of my life. My family came here when I was just a kid. I think my dad was a salesman or something, and came here as part of a promotion for his company. That was a dud. I don't know what happened or why he stayed, really. They bought a little house in town and just stayed. Mom taught school for a few years, and Dad did odd jobs around. He worked out here and I would come with him a lot. When they got older, they moved back to America – Florida. I decided to stay. I got the house and had enough work here to keep me. I used to do all kinds of stuff here, loading and unloading, fixing and stuff, then one day, the guy who had the job I now have, handed me the clipboard and left. I've been doing it ever since."

"So, who do you work for?" Sam queried.

"No one, really. I mean, I guess I work for myself. I never thought about it much."

"What do you mean? Don't you have a boss or the owner of the building or whatever?"

"Nope, the building is just here – don't know that it belongs to anybody. I use it and take care of it and all, but otherwise, it is just here."

"So who manages all of the shipping?" Sam was fascinated.

"Sam, I guess you may have found that things are different here – don't know how they are where you come from, but people don't worry about those kind of things here. It is just Whahilia". (there was that word again!)

"Here is how it is: I am here most every day. A ship comes in, ties up, somebody off the ship says, 'I got some cargo.' I check it to make sure it is for somebody here and sign for it. I take it in and put it in the warehouse. I pay for the stuff and they leave, like you saw today. I'll make a list and then send one of my guys to notify everyone that their stuff is here. They come after it or we deliver and they pay me. I charge for the service."

"Hmmm, so that is it." Sam mused.

"Yup, not a big deal, Sam." Barry chuckled.

"So that is all there is to the whole harbor? Sam asked.

"Oh, no. There is the fuel and stuff - Down there." He pointed to the huge tanks near the area where Sam had seen the private boats. "I don't have anything to do with that, but we get tankers in here to deliver gas and oil. There is a guy down there who handles that. There is a mechanic down there too, who works on cars and boats when there is a need. He keeps pretty busy with the local boaters, I guess. There are a few people on the island that go out fishing or sailing. He helps them some."

Sam was intrigued. He hadn't really thought much about the activities on the island besides the downtown area. But Barry seemed comfortable sharing, so Sam encouraged him on with new questions.

"Where does the gas and electric come from?" He asked.

"You mean, for the houses and such?"

"Yeah."

"Well, all the gas comes from propane, like I suspect you have in your place. People don't use much so it isn't a big deal, the tanks are just replaced when you run out. That comes from down there." Again, indicating the other end of the harbor. "The electric is different. We are on an island co-op that takes care of electric and water and sewer. There is couple of guys who take care of it. We each pay a few bucks a month to keep it taken care of. The water comes from a flowing well up in the hills. The electric comes from a generator up the hill above the town. We used to not have any electric. That is pretty new. Folk got tired of no refrigerators and using lamps so they got together and brought in this big generator. I don't know how it works, but there's wires from it to each house. Most folks got wired up. It was a pretty big deal. The Co-op pays for it. Sewer? I don't know, It goes to some settling pond someplace and then to the ocean, I guess. I think the hotel has it's own system for lights and sewer and the whole thing. You gotta remember, Sam, we are not a big city and most people like it that way." We don't need nothin' modern."

Barry looked wistfully off toward the hills. "I went to Sydney, once. – all the lights and cars, and noise, and stuff. We don't need that here." He sat suddenly silent, eyes closed and hands clasped over his stomach.

Sam took the cue and rose to leave. "Thanks, Barry. It has been nice talking to you. I appreciate the information about Brian. Have a good day." He started to reach out to shake his hand, but could see that Barry was far away in his thoughts. Sam walked away, and back toward town.

Chapter 17

When Sam returned to town, he stopped at the airport to see what he had to do to schedule his return ticket home. It had been an open ticket, paid for, but no date set. There was a lady at the desk, but she didn't know how to schedule such a flight. She told him to 'return tomorrow with his ticket.' He agreed.

Sam stopped in town at the grocery store for a loaf of bread (he had really learned to enjoy the homemade bread of the island). and picked up a couple of items that would fit in a bag. He didn't mention his talk with Barry. Bob didn't ask. After his talk with Barry, he had really begun to understand how isolated the island was and how much its inhabitants liked it that way.

As Sam started for home, he stopped at the art display to admire, again, Kat's works, noticed Gimmie sitting on the bench at the barber shop, and waved at Antoinetta, who was talking to a customer on her front porch; and continued on.

As he was leaving town, the sky turned dark and Sam hurried to the nearby church for shelter from the tropical rain which he had learned would quickly follow. He was glad the church was open, but suddenly felt a little strange in its emptiness. He felt a sudden urge to pray, so with the sound of the rain on the metal roof of the church, he bowed his head and said a prayer for Kat. The rain, as usual, was brief, but he was glad to be still dry, and felt better for the prayer.

At home, Sam went, again to his list, still laying on the table. He noted that he still had not made a definite choice on paper, but he knew he had to go home. Laying the pad aside, he stepped out to, again, drink in the beautiful seascape before him. "I wish Mary could see this." He said aloud, then smiled to himself at what he had just said. "I have to go home and see her." He declared. "I hope she will be there." Finally, he knew the decision was made. He would return. He would face the farm and his future there – not here, five thousand miles away. He would conquer his fears and do what needed to be done. He didn't know what it might be or how to approach it, but his mind was made up. He hadn't seen Kat for a couple days. He supposed she was off painting and he had a lot on his mind so hadn't bothered to look for her. He had to let her know that he was leaving the island. He assumed that she knew that and was conditioning herself to go back to her normal life. He felt sad for her, hating to leave her alone; and his own heart was breaking for what he felt for her. He had to talk to her. He had had no luck in finding answers to her father's disappearance, but decided to not tell her of his attempt. – just to see her and find a way to tell her of his decision.

Kat sat alone on the sand facing the sea. It was the same spot that she and Chad had been on that birthday night, those many years ago. She recounted in her mind those events. – the events of that night and all the things that had followed. – how she had tried to accept it all and had hardened herself, her emotions, her relations, to keep from being hurt. She recalled how she had slowly found a life without people and became comfortable with it. She enjoyed her painting. It was all that was left of her father. He had given her the paints and encouraged her to use her talent – first to help her mother with the pottery and more and more in her own artwork. She had helped her mother; the pottery was their source of income. When her mother left, she continued with her own artwork. She carried her paint box with her and reacted to her surroundings, by painting what she saw. She painted on driftwood, rocks, shells, leaves. She took some of her work to Jaun's shop in town where her mother's pottery was sold and he offered to sell it for her. Jaun didn't talk much, but she could tell he liked it. He seemed to understand it and carefully put it on display for her. She knew he was fair; she trusted him. He would pay her from the sales as he had the pottery. He helped her purchase paint supplies and canvases. She found a satisfaction in her work. She found that she could release her emotions through the brush and paint. That was more important than any money she received from it. It became her life.

Today, as she sat alone, recounting the past events, she remembered often sitting on the steps of the cottage, when it was unoccupied, where Sam now stayed, half-wishing someone lived inside that she could talk to. It was a private, pleasant place where she could watch the sunset on the water and be alone. Then Sam had appeared and she had tried to keep a distance, but also satisfy her curiosity. They had met and it had been a whirlwind of change for her – talking and sharing her island. Now, he was leaving. He hadn't said so, specifically, but she knew it was coming. She had expected it. He had said that he was only there for a little while… Kat was suddenly overtaken with the thought of being alone again. She had become so comfortable with the few days with Sam, it seemed almost impossible to return to the life she had before she met him. She knew she shouldn't care for him the way she did, but she wished he could stay. She wished this feeling that she had for him could continue forever. As she remembered the pain of losing her father and then her mother - and Chad, she erupted in anger.

"I can't go through that again." She said aloud, clenching her fists and pushing them deep into the sand at her sides. "I just can't! It isn't fair!

Then she felt herself in tears – uncontrollably, caught up in a frustrated feeling of loneliness, sadness and bewilderment. She wrapped her arms around her legs with her face pressed onto her knees and wept – and prayed.

Kat was still sobbing when someone touched her shoulder. "Kat" a voice said. And repeated, "Kat . . .?"

She looked up, startled, wiping her eyes, and wiping them again trying to focus. It was Chad! It was Chad – much older looking and more muscular, but it was he. She was speechless.

Chad sat down beside her, slowly speaking, "Kat, It is me. I have been looking for you. I have some things to tell you. – And I have come to ask you to leave the island with me."

Kat, stunned with surprise, sat staring at him, then stammered, "What . . .What are you doing here? Where did you come from?" She didn't know what else to say.

He repeated, "I want you to leave the island with me." I want you to go to Australia with me." He then went on in quick sentences of explanation, "I was working on a ship for over a year. When the ship went into Sydney, Australia, I left the ship and found a good job there. I went looking for your mother. I found her. She is doing well. She would love to see you. I bought a house. It would be perfect for you. I

would like you to come back and live there with me."
He took her hand and looked pleadingly into her eyes.

Kat's mind was swirling. "But it has been so long." she stammered. "I thought I would never see you again." She looked past him, into space as though collecting her thoughts and trying to make sense of it all.

"I know, I know. I shouldn't have left you the way I did, but I took that job on that ship and it just never came back to Pangatango. But, Kat, I never stopped thinking of you. When I found your mother, I promised that I would bring you to her."

Kat, still reeling from the surprise, sat, silent, staring at Chad. Neither spoke for a time, then slowly, Kat reached out to touch him, as though to confirm that he was real, that she was not dreaming. Cautiously, she embraced him and pulled him to her. "It has been a long time." She whispered. He took her in his arms and held her quivering body. They sat in a warm embrace for a long time. Neither spoke.

Finally, Kat sat back, releasing her embrace and started asking questions.

"What are you talking about?

"Leave Pangatango?

"Is this really real?

How would we go?

What about my house here?

What do I need to do?

When do you want me to go?

You saw my mother?"

Chad jumped up, laughing. "We can leave right away. – But if you need time, it can wait a few days. We can fly to Sydney. Anything else you need to take, we can ship."

"But this is my home. I wouldn't know how to live any place else."

"You will learn; and you could come back here to visit sometime, if you wanted to."

Chad stood and pulled Kat to her feet. He held her for a moment in his arms, then repeated, excitedly, "I want you to come and live with me. The house is neat. It is near the water. It has a room that would be a great studio for you. – And it is close to your mother. You could see her every day."

Kat was overwhelmed. "Give me time to think."

"Ok, but not too long. I have to get back to my job."

"Where are you staying?"

"I am staying with Billy. You remember him? We used to play at his house sometimes."

"I guess I remember. I don't talk to people much anymore."

"Yeah, you probably heard that Mom and Dad moved to Sydney after I left here. That is one reason I went there. – So I am staying at Billy's house here for a few days. - But I will tell you all about it. Just make up your mind and come with me. I have some things to do. I will be back for your answer soon."

With that, Chad squeezed Kat's hand briefly and left, leaving Kat standing there in a bit of a stupor. She watched him jog away across the sand and disappear over the dune. Her mind was reeling. Had she just had a dream? Did Chad REALLY just ask her to go live with him? . . . Leave the island and go live with him? It was all so sudden. What should she do?

Then she remembered Sam. She had to talk to Sam. She turned to walk to his house, then broke into a run along the beach to Sam's house. Her thoughts racing, she didn't know how she would tell him. She didn't want to leave him – but he was leaving anyway – what would he say . . .? Her excitement grew in the anticipation of what lay ahead with Chad, but it was mixed with an already developing sadness of losing Sam.

Nearly out of breath, she bounced up the steps of Sam's house calling, "Sam!, Sam!" and stopped on his door step, waiting for a response. There was no answer. "Where could he be? I have to talk to him!"

As Kat sat wondering, Sam appeared, coming from her house where he had been looking for her! Almost in unison, they both said, "I have to talk to you. . ." They laughed, but it was an uncomfortable laugh because both thought the topic would not be an easy one.

Kat spoke first and blurted out. "Sam, Chad came back! He wants me to leave the island with him. What am I going to do?"

She appeared to be so uncertain and confused, that Sam didn't know how to answer. He stood taken aback for a moment, then asked, "Are you going?"

"I don't know. He says he wants me to go to Australia with him. He has seen my mother. He says he has a house and wants me to go live there."

Quickly, Sam grasped the story and encouraged her to go. "It sounds great, Kat!" You can see your mother, AND Chad! I am happy for you. When will you leave?"

Kat was still a little unsure of what to do, and stammered a little. "I don't know, Sam. It is so sudden. I didn't even know Chad was here. He just appeared and asked me to go with him. What should I do? - What about you, Sam? What will you do?" She wanted to tell him that she didn't want to leave him, but hid her thoughts.

Sam tried to not let his feelings show, but finally said, "Kat, I was going to tell you that I have decided to leave. I didn't want to leave you alone, but this is perfect. It is like a miracle for you. You won't be alone when I leave." He reached out and hugged her and they both laughed. Kat cried. Sam hugged her tighter. "I want to meet Chad." He said at last. "Come, let's talk about it"

They moved to the place that had been their most comfortable place – the steps of the house, facing the sea - and broke into a conversation about how they both had a new life ahead of them. Sam started with "You won't believe this, but I went to the church and prayed for you – and you have received a miracle!"

Kat, looked at him in disbelief. "You prayed? I prayed too! I was so upset and confused that I just prayed to God to help. He heard our prayers!" Yes, it was a miracle! They could both be happy.

Over and over they exclaimed to each other how it had all been like an answer from Heaven – at the same time!

Then Sam shared how he had made his decision and was leaving in a few days to go back and face his future, hoping Mary would be there to share it with him. Kat slowly began to gain excitement about seeing her mother again and being with Chad again.

While they were talking, Chad appeared. "I have been looking for you!" He declared. "What are you doing here?"

Kat rose to meet him, excitedly. "Hi Chad! I want you to meet Sam. He is staying here from America."

Sam rose and extended his hand. "Hello, Chad. I have heard a lot about you. I understand you are taking Kat to Australia."

Chad shook his hand. "Glad to meet you. Yes, I am hoping she will go with me to live in Sydney. How long have you been here? What part of America are you from? Are you staying long?"

Sam explained briefly that he was on a little vacation from Iowa and was only there for a few weeks and would be leaving in a few days. He again, shared that he was glad that Kat would be able to see her mother again.

Chad turned his attention to Kat. "Have you decided?"

"YES!" she replied excitedly. I was just telling Sam how great it will be. When do we need to go? Will you help me gather my things?"

"Sure, right away. Let's go to your house and gather your things. Can you leave tomorrow?"

"I guess so. It is all so sudden."

"No problem, I really don't want to rush you; maybe day after tomorrow. Lets pack and then I will go get our tickets."

"Nice talking to you, Chad." Sam said as he watched them on the path toward Kat's house. "I hope we can talk again before you leave." He settled again on the step and watched the waves and the gulls, marveling at all that had happened and how the pieces of his struggle had all seemed to come together.

Chapter 18

Sam woke early. It was to be his last day on Pangatango. He decided to walk the beach again one more time. He started out recounting the memories of the past few weeks. He couldn't even remember how many weeks that had been. Time had been lost somehow. The events all seemed to run together in his mind as he followed the same sandy beach that he had walked so many times. He reached the now familiar cliff and smiled at how he had seen footsteps disappear here and then learned the answer to the mystery.

"One more time." He said aloud and plodded through the water and rocks to the hidden opening in the rock. He climbed the steep ramp that he and Kat had climbed several times. They had scrambled to the top of the cliff, laughing and playing like two carefree children. This time it was not a laughing race. He struggled with each painful step, remembering her feet in front of him on those same rocks as he had followed her up the steep incline and her laughter when she reached the top ahead of him only to turn and reach out her hand for him. At the top, they had settled in exhaustion and watched the sea together. This time, he edged slowly to the place where they had sat watching the dolphins below. He stood alone overlooking the ocean. His mind raced over the events of the last few weeks. He embraced the wind that brought him the smells and sounds of the ocean. He wanted to drink in every part of it. He didn't want to lose the feeling that it gave. Below the sea crashed incessantly on the rocks. He looked down at the foam and swirling waters as over and over the waves tried to penetrate the unwavering fortress of solid rock – like the struggle that had crashed within him over and over, seemingly meaningless and eternal. His eyes searched the surrounding waters for the familiar fins of the dolphins, but found none. He stood alone and felt an emptiness that made him want to scream to the sea.

His heart ached for the feelings he had for Kat, but his mind reminded him that these were not the feelings he wanted. He wanted her companionship, physically, not romantically. He wanted the carefree happiness that he felt when he was with her, but he knew those things were temporary and that eventually he would have to face the reality of the things that had sent him to Pangatango in the first place. He had not come to Pangatango to find a lover. He had not come to Pangatango to begin a new life away from the one that he knew at home. He had come to escape the distractions of a life that was closing in around him. He had come to be alone and to think and resolve his questions. Strangely he had found himself with new questions and new distractions. The past weeks with Kat had lifted a heavy load from his mind and replaced it with new outlooks on life. Now he wanted to go home! He had had his time of solitude. He had had his time of introspection. Kat had opened up a part of him that he had lost many years ago. He still had decisions to make, but he was ready. The ache he had struggled with for Kat softened to the memory of something so wonderfully sweet that it made him smile, and replacing it was an ache for home. Pangatango had been good for him. He had found what he had come all these miles looking for – and more. He found that he had been able to laugh. He had been able to put his feelings into perspective and live with emotions that had been gripping him. He knew that Kat also had had feelings, but Chad had come home and was taking her to Australia. He had bought a house there, with a studio for Kat. It overlooked the sea and it was close to the place where her mother was living. Kat would be able to spend much time recovering the relationship that she thought was lost forever. Knowing that she would be happy relieved the sadness he felt in leaving her.

Descending, he walked the final long trek back to his cottage – on the familiar sand, seaweed, shells, and small stones that he had seen beneath his feet over and over - past the driftwood he had sat on, the dunes where he had shared long talks with Kat, past the area of the Pango village, noticing a boat in the water a distance from the beach. He waved at the man in the boat but got no response. Finally, reaching his own door step, he paused and sat to drink it in one more time. Tomorrow he would leave all of this behind.

Sam's thoughts were interrupted by the appearance of Kat and Chad. She was carrying her paint box and a large tote bag. Chad was also burdened with bags. – all of Kat's possessions, Sam assumed.

"We are leaving." Kat announced, excitedly, but with a sadness in her eyes.

Chad turned to talk to Sam. Kat walked away and left them alone. "Sam," he started, "I wish we could talk more. Kat has told me about you and how you came here to get away from the world. It is a good place to do that. I think your being here has helped Kat, too. She has been alone for too long. I should never have left her, but I will take care of her now."

"I know you will, Chad. It is so great that you found her mother and can take her there." Sam looked to see that Kat was not nearby and quickly said, "I tried to find some information about her father, but had no luck. Maybe you can find out what happened to him."

"I will try."

Sam handed him a card with his address on it. "Let me know." He said.

Kat returned, gave Sam a hug and said good-bye. Chad shook his hand again and wished him well.

Sam watched them walk toward town, and called after them, "Good luck, be happy!"

Chapter 19

Sam walked slowly along the road that he had walked many times. He had opted to walk the road to town one more time. He wanted to leave the island one step at a time. He was leaving, but there was no need to rush. The plane would not leave for hours yet and it felt good to take his time. A cool breeze came from the sea and he could hear the crashing of the waves. He could hear the gulls taunting, tempting him to stay, but he had no ears for their pleading. He listened to his own footsteps on the road and watched the breeze cause the leaves overhead to flutter their goodbyes. His thoughts were of home. He remembered the farm, retracing footsteps from building to building in his mind. He remembered the smell of the fields in the spring and the rustle of the corn leaves in summer. He remembered his mother's dying words to take care of the farm - and he remembered Mary. He had many thoughts of Mary. He wanted very much to explain why he had left. He wanted to make her understand why he had left, but more importantly why he had returned. He wanted to return the love and devotion that he had seen in her eyes day after day toward his mother and toward him. It was a love he hadn't understood then but wanted to see and feel again.

He felt a need to say good-by to Antoinetta, and to Bob. He didn't want to talk long or explain, but he didn't want to leave without at least thanking them for their hospitality. He knew that they were 'island people' and would continue to live their lives one day at a time. His stay had not made an impact on their lives and his leaving would not; but he felt a warmth toward them and wanted to express it in a good-bye. They each cordially wished him well. He gave them each his address, but didn't expect to ever hear from them. He didn't stop to inspect the paintings as he usually did, assuming that Kat had taken them with her when she left. He just continued on to the airport to sit on that bench and wait for his plane.

There was no crowd of well-wishers at the airport – just a routine checking of tickets and loading of a few suitcases and when all was on board, no loud announcement, or fan-fare. The pilot revved the engines, and the plane taxied to the end of the runway and then turned and took off. They made a wide circle around the island as they rose to flight elevation and Sam watched through the tiny window as the island grew smaller and smaller below him - The beaches, the palms, the tiny town and harbor – and the towering volcano mountain . . . . . slowly disappeared in a veil of misty clouds - like a dream slowly fading as one wakens in the morning.

As he settled in his seat, Sam thought of the long flight ahead of him. He reached into the bag at his feet, poking through his few clothes that he had thrown in at the last minute, for his almost forgotten crosswords book and felt something else. Kat had apparently put something in his bag while he was talking to Chad. He pulled out a loosely wrapped package with Kat's name and an Australia address on it. He carefully opened it to find a small painting - of Sam's cottage with a basket of fruit on the doorstep. – and another small box which, when he opened it, revealed some shiny seashells and a note saying 'Don't forget them this time.'

Epilogue

Mary walked uncertainly toward Sam as he emerged from the plane's ramp. He was so handsome and strong looking. His face and arms so tan…She almost didn't recognize him. His hair was much longer. He was thinner and seemed to stand taller. She stopped when their eyes met and managed a smile. They stood only for a minute and then hurriedly came together. Sam dropped his bag and swept her into his arms, lifting her from the floor and holding her for a long moment suspended and out of breath. When he finally allowed her to stand, it was with unsteady feet. She had never felt anything like it. Her blood raced. Her hair tingled and it seemed the world had stopped.

"How did you know I would be here?" Sam asked.

"I have been watching every day for two months."

She reached out for his hand, wondering what to expect. He took hers with a confident assurance that he was ready for whatever life held for the two of them – together.

Printed in the United States
By Bookmasters